Sounds of Home

Debbie Boyle

~For Mom and Dad, who created a childhood that I still dream about and who believed that I could do anything.

ACKNOWLEDGMENTS

For always encouraging me to keep writing, I would like to thank, Tom, Danni, Riley, Jessi, Kit, Jim, Cindy, Dan, Janet, Linda, Bob, Sandy, Dan, the Boyle Family, and my many nieces and nephews, cousins, and lifelong friends. Tyler, thank you for your hours of proofreading. Rowe, Crew, and all future grandchildren, thank you for keeping me young. Mrs. Holt, my Fifth Grade Teacher, your love of music inspired my love of school. To my neighbors- Warren Street   Forever!

PROLOGUE

2017

It was like watching a treasured family heirloom crushed beneath the sole of a boot. A cloud of dust wafting through the chain link barrier smelled of musty old books and chalk. It lingered like perfume after its owner had long before vacated the area. Brick after brick, I winced as each mini bomb exploded on the blacktop below. I scanned the ground looking for one brick relic unaffected by the giant yellow dinosaur who appeared to be devouring the beloved old building for its noon-time meal, but there were none. The brontosaurus took another giant bite, and I eased myself down to the curb as a gaping hole revealed the faint yellow wall of my fifth-grade classroom.

"Nana, dat's a big mess!" my grandson's wide

eyes turned toward me, a chubby finger pointing through a link in the fence at the chunk of plaster that had broken free and tumbled onto the pile of crumbled bricks.

"Yes, that is a big mess," I pulled my knees up to rest my chin on my folded arms.

He turned back and watched wide-eyed, little fingers clinging to the fence, as the giant excavator gouged chunk after chunk, soon erasing the whole north wall of the building.

An old-timer stood in the shade of a tree shaking his head. "I went to school there, back in the 30's. Boy, we had some good times in that old school," and he let out a deep sigh. "Yes, it's a real shame," his voice trailed off as he pulled a faded tweed newsboy cap over the remaining gray hairs on his head. After a final look at the school, he turned and disappeared into the crowd.

Other people were milling about and reminiscing about the good old days. Their basset hound eyes blinking as though they were watching their best friend pack up and move away. They had fought to save the iconic landmark, but the battle was over, leaving them to witness a piece of their history vanishing before their eyes.

Amid the brick bombardment, a single piece of paper fluttered from the classroom, bypassing the construction equipment, wafting like a bird's feather on the breezes until it landed inside the fence near the feet of my grandson. He squatted down to investigate. "Nana, birdie! Look a birdie!" He was doing his best to get a closer look, pressing his cheek against the metal so one eyeball could get a better view through a link in the fence.

I eyed the picture at his feet. The sun-bleached artwork revealed a paper mosaic in the shape of a bird, maybe an eagle or an osprey. I reached under the fence to slide the picture out. In the lower right-hand corner, a faint signature, *Danny*, was written in perfect cursive.

"Why, yes, you are right! It is a bird, maybe an osprey?" I put an arm around my grandson.

"Pwetty!" he grinned.

"It sure is," I whispered. He turned to watch the dinosaur through the fence as I sat down and examined the artwork. Holding it up to the sun, I squinted at the osprey, imagining it in flight over the playground, jarring a memory from another lifetime when an osprey had found its home near our playground. I squinted to read faint writing below Danny's name and bolted upright as a date came into focus, *June 2, 1970*, a true artifact from the previous century.

The fact that this piece of paper had survived for that many years, probably stuck in some crack between a cupboard and a wall, or an old filing cabinet, was one thing, but 1970? That was nearly fifty years ago, my fifth-grade year.

I laughed thinking that this was too much of a coincidence. "No way," I squinted again at the date, recalling a Danny O'Boyle, who sat behind me in Mrs. Holt's class.

"What Nana?" my grandson looked at me.

"Oh, nothing, buddy," a goofy smile erupted, and I laughed out loud, but then instantly struggled to swallow a lump that had formed in my throat.

It had been forty-seven years since that summer of 1970 when my life was turned inside out, but it seemed like yesterday...

CHAPTER 1

1970

Jesse was missing, at least that was what everyone believed, even the government for that matter. But, ten-year-olds in this town were better at keeping secrets than most people would think.

Never, would I have imagined that the events of a world so far away from my sleepy little town, could weave their way into our Norman Rockwell existence that summer, changing the fabric of my neighborhood. For those ten-year-olds, oh, and yes, the young at heart, impossibilities became truth and the unbelievable became believable. By the time the budding greens of spring evolved to the golden grasses of summer, I would be racing to save my sister, and grieving the loss of a friend.

5

Some would call it an act of courage, but that does not mean I wasn't afraid.

It was the summer of 1970 and the world was mourning the breakup of the Beatles. Their final album, *Let it Be,* played as a definitive piece of advice to the world, while the never-ending Vietnam War raged on our console TV.

The Jackson Five had made their national debut on Dick Clark's *American Bandstand.* It was holy church on Saturday mornings in our house, and Dick Clark, the preacher. Sonny and Cher, The Jackson Five, and The Beach Boys served as members of the prestigious choir, and I sang their praises from the shag carpet in my living room.

Clearly, our Warren Street house was on the opposite end of the spectrum from the mansions of anyone who dared to live their dreams out on Saturday morning TV. But it was a magnificent mansion, according to my six-year-old self at first glance, since it had a second floor. After living in "the cracker box," my mom's term for the tiny house into which our family of eight had been crammed into prior to Warren Street, I ran through this new delight yelling, "We live in a mansion! We live in a mansion!"

Our "new" house had been built in 1912. The covered front porch served as a pirate ship during summer rainstorms and an enemy prison for neighborhood games like Kick the Can. Apple trees and purple lilac bushes saturated the springtime air with their fragrance and created a shady back yard oasis during hot summer months. Unfortunately, the house also came with 1912 plumbing, and an electrical system that didn't collaborate with the power needed for modern vacuum cleaners, clothes dryers, or electric mixers. It was expected that fuses would be blown during holiday gatherings when every electrical appliance revved at full capacity.

Built in a historical section of town, our house sat three blocks down from St. Helena's, a towering cathedral perched on a hill overlooking downtown Helena. Modeled after the Gothic cathedrals in Europe, people came from all over to attend mass and get photos of Helena's grandest architectural masterpiece.

St. Helena's Cathedral had been constructed by an Irish immigrant, who had once slept on the streets of Helena at first arrival to the booming mining town. Like many others in the community, he became a millionaire when he struck it rich mining for gold, but he donated his riches to begin constructing St. Helena's Cathedral for the people of the town. Sadly, his was the first funeral to be held in the exquisite house of worship. The Cathedral would play a part in the events that jostled our neighborhood that summer.

My best friend, Jilly, lived three houses up the street from me, and we were like sisters. Our first meeting happened one September evening, when there was a bit of a ruckus in our back yard. My family had only been living in the new house for a week when the previous owners came back to reap the harvest of the three apple trees that they had so lovingly tended over the summer. Running their plan for an evening harvest by my parents had slipped the former homeowners' minds, and they thought we wouldn't notice the lack of apples on our trees when we woke up the next morning.

Jilly's family provided moral support for the apple

thieves, and rightfully so since they had enjoyed their neighborhood friendship for a decade. There was an exchange of words, but my parents were never big on confrontation and decided to listen to the advice of the Beatles, and let it be. We would have no applesauce that fall.

During that neighborhood meeting, I had noticed a little girl with long brown hair, who looked to be about my age standing next to her mom. We had a brief stare down, and sized each other up, each wondering if the other was friend material. We officially met a few days later when she came to our front door asking my sister, Winnie, and me if we wanted to play Kick the Can with the rest of the neighborhood. We happily agreed, and thus was the beginning of a friendship that endured decades.

CHAPTER 2

June 1970 brought the last day of fifth grade before summer vacation. Jilly and I raced the twelve gongs of the Cathedral bells four blocks home for lunch. Our trip back to school included a detour to the Hi Tri, a small triangular shaped café on Helena Avenue, that was just big enough to hold a lunch counter.

Miss Rosie, the waitress at the Hi-Tri, was a 50's caricature from the set of an Elvis movie. She had worked at the Hi-Tri for as long as we had been going there to load up on bubblegum and Reese's Cups. Hair shellacked with Dippity-Do, ratted and pinned into a beehive style, we thought it would have made a nice home for a family of mice or some homeless spiders. Rhinestone cat-eyeglasses that had enough sparkle to signal an airplane overhead if the sun's angles hit them just right were leashed around her neck by an equally bedazzled chain. The chain's purpose was purely decorative since the frames of her glasses were held tight between her concrete hair and ear.

Wads of pink bubblegum softened in our mouths

as we made our way back to school. We were not allowed to chew gum in school, so our chewed wads were stored in the pencil trays inside our desks. No attention was paid to the fact that the desk had been used by generations of students before us, and probably contained enough germs to be a science experiment in Louis Pasteur's lab. When I lifted the lid of my desk, the delectable, sweet smell of the bubblegum would overtake my senses, and I couldn't resist sticking the pink mass onto the roof of my mouth. Great skill was needed to read about Amerigo Vespucci's voyage aloud in class, with a wad of gum stuck on the roof of your mouth, but we were masters at it, or so we thought. I'm sure Mrs. Holt chose her battles and decided to ignore our gum obsession. Reciting from our Social Studies book, *"Amerigo Vesh-pooshi shet shail in 1499,"* was at least proof we could read.

Central school was an amazing old stone and brick building, built in the early 1900's, that had somehow survived the great earthquake of 1935. Citizens of Helena took pride in the fact that Central School stood as one of the first graded schools in Montana. With its collegiate architecture and Gothic flair, it was a prominent landmark nestled amid the nearby Cathedral and downtown structures in its neighborhood.

Central was built next door to an old high school that had been damaged in the quake yet remained standing because the townspeople were at odds with each other whether to tear it down or not. It was a towering, dark stone, castle-like structure, that loomed like a sentry over our elementary school. Its windows and doors had been boarded up for some time, giving it a very spooky presence. Passing it each day to get to school took a feat of courage and a Jesse Owens' sprint from corner to corner, too fast for any ominous tenant to whisk us into its lair.

Even more eerie, the condemned high school had been built on the site of the old city cemetery. Of course, the remains from the cemetery had been relocated to the valley long before both schools were built on the grounds, but there had been a perpetual, lingering rumor concerning one miner's grave that had been forgotten beneath the school grounds.

Kids in the area were certain, the ghost of the dead miner was still meandering around the old high school, which made for thrilling double dares during recess. We would play Rock–Paper–Scissors to see who would dash up the steps of the high school and touch the door without being murdered, by whatever figment of our imaginations lived inside. Like it or not, Jilly, my three sisters, and I, would have to face our fears that summer, and the old high school would give up one of its secrets.

On the other hand, inside nearby Central School, worries about ghosts and graves would disappear. Laughing children would drown out any speculations of ghostly chains rattling, or moans and groans coming from an unwanted specter in search of their gold. Thousands of pairs of shoes had shuffled over Central's golden wood floors through the years, from lace up boots to Mary Jane's, to saddle shoes and penny loafers. Whatever era, most students of Central Elementary School will tell you that the school had some type of magical hold over each person who walked its hallowed halls and spoke fondly of the old building as if it were a dear family member. Central School was a much beloved part of our community.

High ceilings and walls with bright bulletin boards lined the hallways. Tall windows welcomed the sunlight and provided inspiring views of Mount Helena during the golden colors of fall, the soft falling snows of winter, and the carpet of yellow arrow leaf on the mountain's eastern slope that bloomed in the much-awaited spring.

Jilly and I were ecstatic when we read the class list on the front door the week before school started, and found we were both in Mrs. Holt's fifth grade class. Mrs. Holt played the piano every day and we cherished singing along each morning before starting lessons. Our classroom would be transformed into Woody Guthrie's America as we melded harmonies and melodies of *This Land is Your Land* and *Roll-on Columbia.*

Mrs. Holt also played the piano for every Central School Christmas program, extravaganzas that were traditionally aired on the local radio station. The fifth and sixth graders practiced for weeks, working on harmonies that complimented the melodies, creating an angelic choir of voices for *O Holy Night, Silver Bells,* and *Silent Night.* The kids in my class gladly sacrificed math and spelling, to practice for the program in the rafters of the Seventh Avenue Gym.

Mrs. Pare directed, demanding we stand with our hands clasped over our stomachs with eyes following her every move. She was not our regular music teacher, but a sixth-grade teacher, who we believed had been a drill sergeant in her former life. She scared the living crap out of us, and I secretly prayed to God, Jesus, and the Holy Mother that I would not be in her class the following year.

It wasn't until I became a teacher myself, that I realized the pressure the teachers were under to produce a spectacular Christmas program. The local radio station would record our program and air it during the holidays, for the whole town to enjoy, so we practiced and practiced until there were no mistakes. In the end, even though the process was grueling, students and teachers took great pride in knowing we had created a memory that would last a lifetime.

It was experiences like being part of the Central School Christmas program that we treasured. It was a sense of belonging, and creating something beautiful, even though we were wearing hand me down clothes and bread bags inside our boots to keep out the snow. We could relate to *The Little Match Girl,* a Central School Christmas tradition, and felt great empathy for the main character, a young girl who dies on a cold winter day, trying desperately to earn money for her family. The moral of the story dug deep, and we learned to be grateful and happy for what we were given.

Now, here we were, the final day in Mrs. Holt's fifth grade class. Our common bond being the love of music, and I would cherish her daily musical rituals for the rest of my life. I had to admit I was probably the only kid who was sad it was the last day of fifth grade. Who knew which teacher I would have the following year in sixth grade, it made my stomach churn.

I was contemplating my sixth-grade future and gluing pieces of paper to a poster sized mosaic, our final project of the year that was supposed to represent the American spirit. What could represent Americana more than the greatest band that ever lived, The Beach Boys? Unfortunately, Dennis Wilson was taking on more of a resemblance to a frightened cat with a unibrow and his brother, Brian, a blob holding a guitar.

In reaching for the glue, I happened to glance

down from our second story classroom window, and spied a dog that looked much like mine, wandering the school grounds. As I followed its path, I realized it indeed was my dog, Skip.

Skip would jump our six-foot fence and follow us to school on a regular basis. He also detested men and boys alike. Skip showed his disdain for my brothers' friends, by nipping them on the backs of their legs or hind ends at any swift movement. Inevitably, after their initial meeting with Skip, the skittish boys would try to sneak past him and make a break for it up the stairs to my brothers' room. Before we could tell them not to run, their yelps and cuss words could be heard throughout the house after receiving Skip's permanent teeth impressions in their heels and behinds.

Skip had been a stray mutt that "followed" us home from Memorial Park one day. He would have gone unnoticed had we been in a field of summer wheat except for his shiny black nose which happened to be the perfect height to nudge my hand for a pet. His caramel-colored eyes caught my attention and instantly melted my heart. He was a little skittish though when we tried to approach him at that first meeting and dodged and darted away thinking he was playing a game with us. But with some coaxing and promises of a piece of cookie along with a jump rope lassoed around his neck, he came willingly.

My parents were not thrilled to see this stray mutt inside the house when they came home from work that day. We had fed him a lunch of Spaghetti-O's and tuna fish sandwiches, so he was not going to leave any time soon. Try as they might, with ads in the local newspaper and calls to the dog shelter, my parents were unable to locate the owners, so Skip became our dog.

Now he was down there in front of the school, sniffing around looking for my six-year-old sister, and me. That dog had an amazing sniffer! If he could detect our scents from the hundreds of other kids who smelled of peanut butter and jelly and old milk, pink bubble gum and glue, he probably should have been working for a police department or some detective agency.

I knew I couldn't call my parents to come get Skip, because they were both at work, and realistically, they wouldn't have minded if Skip found a new home anyway.

I whispered to Jilly, "Skip is down there," and pointed out the window. "What am I gonna do? I won't be able to leave school to take him home!"

"Tell Mrs. Holt you are going to the bathroom and run out and take him home. You can make it there and back in less than ten minutes. If she gets suspicious, I will tell her you think you ate something bad and you need some time," Jilly whispered.

My mind pictured the questioning look on Mrs. Holt's face as she imagined what Jilly meant by me, "needing some time" in the bathroom. "Oh man, I hope she doesn't find out I'm gone. My parents will ground me for a week," I worried.

"Just go, it'll be fine," Jilly reassured me. One thing about Jilly, she always had my back and could instantaneously think of solutions when we got ourselves into a pickle.

Case in point, one day after school, Harvey Dill was up to his same old mean self. He was a royal pain in the you know what, picking on girls and kids who appeared to be weaker than him. Our only saving grace was his short round stature, so chances were probable that we could outrun him. His dark greasy hair hid his eyes from the world. He often came to school in the same clothes that he had worn the previous day, complimented by a black eye or some sort of bruise we all knew, had most likely been delivered by his old man.

He teased me mercilessly about my pixie haircut, reminding me that I looked like a boy. I will admit, I was a tad sensitive about that subject, since my mom wouldn't let me grow my hair long, and people often mistook me for a boy. It didn't help that I hated wearing dresses, either.

But, on this particular day, Harvey was hiding behind the corner of the school and made a surprise attack. He stuck his foot out and tripped me as I ran past him, sending me flying down onto the rough asphalt playground. My hands took the brunt of the tumble and were shredded by small pieces of gravel embedded in both palms. I didn't feel pain, only the anger boiling inside as I sprung up and turned to face Harvey. Swinging my leg as hard I could, I aimed for his private parts. He reacted by jumping out of the way mid-launch. The force of my kick caused my right penny loafer to sail off my foot and land about twenty feet away. Harvey ran and grabbed my shoe, feeling the need to throw it high up into a towering pine tree that stood next to the old haunted high school.

"Uh-oh, your shoe flew into the tree!" Harvey laughed in a high- pitched squeal. His lame imitation of a girl, "I wonder how that happened?" He put both hands on his cheeks, eyes fluttering, trying to appear innocent.

I held up a fist, so wanting to give him a knuckle sandwich, eyes boring a hole into his, as I stormed over to the tree to try and retrieve my shoe. Even though Harvey

Dill deserved a pounding, he had the street smarts to win any school-yard fight, and I was terrified that he would really lose his temper, and more than my shoe would fly into the tree. His dad had taught him well. Everyone in the school was afraid of him, and that included many of the teachers.

But there must have been a full moon in the making, because on this day, it was Jilly who snapped. She finally had enough of Harvey Dill, and decided the proverbial last straw had been thrown onto the camel's back. It was only the day before her bookbag had been launched onto the roof of the Seventh Avenue Gym.

Jilly was rounding the corner of the school when she saw Harvey fling my shoe into the tree. She lurched to a stop, her mouth disappearing into a thin line, eyes transforming into the color of steel. Breathing like a bull getting ready for his eight seconds at the state fair, one finger targeted her victim across the playground, and she screamed, "Harvey Dill, you are dead meat!"

Pigeons perched on the ledge of the school roof fluttered off and the playground became a still life painting, as kids froze, eyes wide and wondering. The anticipation of what was about to happen created a buzz of whispers.

Jilly sprinted like a blood thirsty cheetah toward a paralyzed gazelle. Everyone between her and Harvey Dill stopped to make way for Jilly, like the parting of the Red Sea. More kids came pouring around the corner to see what the commotion was, as she finally caught up with Harvey on the grassy side of the old high school, out of sight from the playground teachers.

A raucous chant echoed between the buildings, "Fight! Fight! Fight!" as Jilly tackled Harvey, preventing him from running for the street. Harvey was caught off guard, never in his wildest dreams did he think a girl would physically fight back. Wrestling him to the ground in her plaid jumper, Jilly didn't seem to notice, or care, that she was wearing a dress. He landed with a loud, "Oomph," face planting into the grass.

"Holy crap!" I gasped, in awe of this miracle happening before my eyes. I screamed, "Get 'em, Jilly!"

They were rolling around on the grass and kids circled around to watch this once in a lifetime event. At one point, Jilly mashed Harvey's face into the grass and gave it one extra shove as she sprang to her feet to face him. He struggled to push himself off the grass and staggered to a stand, blinking his eyes trying to focus. A sprig of grass colored his front teeth. He kept spitting, trying to set it free.

Like a scene from an old John Wayne western, Jilly's eyes lowered to a squint as her right hand balled into a fist. Before we knew it, a knobby fist collided with Harvey's right eye. Stunned, we watched Harvey fall to the ground like a freshly cut Christmas pine.

Silence fell over the crowd as we examined his unmoving corpse at the center of our circle. Jilly yanked Harvey's smelly black Converse off his foot. She proceeded to fling it clear over the stone wall where it landed in the middle of Lawrence Street, and was immediately flattened by a school bus.

Peering down at Harvey whose moans revealed he had come back to life, she cupped her cheek in her hand looking completely innocent, "Oh shoot, was that your shoe that just got run over by the bus? How in the world did that happen?" She spit on the ground next to him as she turned to leave and screamed, "Next time, it will be your head, you miserable jerk!"

With that, she brushed the grass off her knees, smoothed out her jumper, and thrust her balled fists to her sides, releasing an exasperated sigh. A playground of open-mouthed statues watched her calm the wild strands of her long brown hair that had freed from their braids as she turned on her heel to storm away from the school. For one amazing day, there was a new sheriff in town.

So, I knew Jilly would take care of things while I escaped from the school to take Skip home. Slipping out of the classroom, I held my breath and tip-toed down the creaky wooden staircase, trying not to let its old age alert any staff members of my exit plan.

I made it out the side door of the school and began whisper yelling, "Skip! Skip! Come here, boy..." of course he wouldn't come when I called, he never did when he sensed urgency in my voice. I was going to have to use the only tactic that would work with him when he escaped the fence. "Skip! Go to the lake? Go to the lake?" He loved going to the lake on summer weekends, it was his dog heaven. If he thought he was going to the lake, he would come running.

My ploy worked, and he looked up from the source of his sniffing and ran after me the four blocks home down Warren Street to my house. I jumped up the steps of the front porch two at a time, hoping to keep his momentum going, so he didn't get suspicious and realize we weren't getting in a car headed for the lake.

His tail whacked my leg as I struggled to turn the old brass doorknob. Slobber streamed from his pink tongue onto the indoor/outdoor carpeting as his eager eyes looked up at me. He had no idea that he was not going to his Garden of Eden.

Once inside, I knelt to pet the top of his head, touching my cheek to his wet black nose. "Skip, you have to stay here. Sorry, buddy, we can't go to the la..." I didn't want to say the word, because he would just start going bananas again. "You stay, I'll be back soon."

I swear he understood English, because when his brown eyes caught mine, his smile instantly disappeared. His perky ears flattened against his head; droopy tail settled on the rust-colored shag carpet. He would not be chasing seagulls on the sandy beach at the lake today.

I squeezed out the front door, praying he wouldn't tear up the sheer curtains covering the door's window, in his quest to follow me. He had shredded the custom-made curtains once before, trying to save us from the mailman, and my mom blew a major gasket.

I jumped down all five of the front steps at once, and raced back to the school, worrying Mrs. Holt had noticed I was gone. Hopefully, Jilly was covering for me.

I was making my ceremonial dash past the old high school, when something caught the corner of my eye. There was a gap in the board covering one of the second story windows, and I swore something moved past it. My heart skipped a beat and I darted behind a tree, knowing that no one had been in that building for years and years. I shaded my eyes with my hands, to get a better view, and stared at the gap in the board. "Wha-a-at the...? I whispered to myself.

My mind raced, recalling the many stories of the one grave that remained under the old school, and the bad juju that most likely remained. I pictured a ghost moaning and groaning about his stolen gold claim, wandering aimlessly through the abandoned classrooms, vowing to use his pickaxe to defend his property. I prayed he hadn't seen me standing all alone and I would have hugged the tree I was hiding behind until recess, but a horn honked across the street and jolted me into a full sprint back toward the school.

By the time I got to the classroom, I gulped a gallon of water from the fountain and stopped to catch my breath, so Mrs. Holt wouldn't become suspicious. The class had just finished cleaning up from the art project and was milling about the room. Jilly saw me peek in the doorway and motioned for me to come in.

"Betts, you look like you've just seen a ghost!" she whispered. "What's wrong? Couldn't you catch Skip?"

"I did! I-I… I think I just saw a ghost," I put my hand over my mouth to stop more talk of ghosts from coming out of it. Jilly's eyes were wide, and I could see the gears turning in her head.

"Jilly and Elizabeth, please take your seats," Mrs. Holt requested from across the room. We would have to finish the discussion when school was out. Jilly and I gave each other sideways looks and sat down in our desks. It was going to be difficult to concentrate.

The last day of school meant our desks had to be cleaned and scrubbed for the next batch of fifth graders. I wondered if anyone would see my name carved inside a hundred years from now, and wonder, who was *Betts 1970?*

The last five minutes of class, Mrs. Holt gathered us around the piano, and we sang *Auld Lang Syne.* I blinked trying to clear my foggy eyes, so no one would think I was a baby. Most kids couldn't wait to get out of school, but I secretly wished fifth grade wasn't over. I gave Mrs. Holt a hug and thanked her for being my favorite teacher and told her I would miss her. It was the truth. She was a big influence in my decision to study to become a teacher after I graduated high school.

Jilly and I grabbed the remaining items from our desks, including the saved wads of bubblegum, and headed outside, straight toward the old high school.

"I don't see anything," Jilly squinted toward the window, "are you sure it wasn't the reflection from the sun?" She kept squinting toward the window, curving her hands around her eyes like a pair of binoculars. She reached one hand inside her pocket and shoved a used wad of bubblegum in her mouth, all the while staring at the window, but having to take exaggerated chomps at the hardened bubblegum to soften it.

"I don't know, I guess it could have been the sun," I said as I stuffed my own wad of gum into my mouth. My tongue immediately detected a foreign substance, and I spit out a small piece of pencil shaving. We both stared at the window, but there was no sign of movement now. I frowned, and blew a huge bubble, starting to doubt what I had seen.

"Come on, let's go home. Schools out, we're free! Yippee!" Jilly yelled. I chased after her down the street toward our houses, and began to speed past her, each of us trying to outrun the other. We were in a full sprint by the time we hit our block.

We plopped down on the grass in front of Jilly's house. "Geez, you're so competitive," Jilly laughed.

"I don't know about being competitive," I breathed, "I started thinking about the miner's ghost, and the more I thought about him, the faster I ran."

I had been a little on edge anyways, since my experience at the Sky Hi Drive-In the weekend before. My brother, Duke, and Jilly's sister, Jane, thought it would be fun to take Jilly and me to the Sky Hi Drive-In to see the movie, *Night of the Living Dead*. Our sisters, Winnie and Cate joined us, too.

Talk about the scariest night of my life! In the movie, a girl and her brother go to a cemetery on a blustery, gray overcast day. The girl is deathly afraid of cemeteries and can hardly get out of the car when her brother parks the car at the base of a hill, near her parents' graves. When she finally builds the courage to exit the car, as luck would have it, zombie-like dead people start chasing them.

It didn't end well for Johnny, the girl's brother, and he of course, had the keys to the car. She ends up being trapped in an old farmhouse with zombies moaning and groaning and pounding on the doors. I was screaming and hiding my face, paralyzed with fear, hoping we would make it home alive from the drive-in.

Jilly and I still had fresh petrifying thoughts in our heads from that movie, so we were on high alert for things like ghosts and zombies. I was so scared that living dead people were going to bust out of their graves and take over our town, I had to sleep with the light on every night, much to the dismay of Winnie, and my six-year-old sister, Roo, since I shared a room with them. Tonight, would be no different.

CHAPTER 3

My older sister, Winnie, had to keep an eye on Roo and me during the summer months while my parents were working. She typically did most of the cleaning since I wouldn't participate in household chores without a stubborn protest. There was no payment for this position, even though Winnie had to be on high alert with Roo around.

Roo was christened Marguerite Ann, named after my grandmother, but after identifying with the adorable baby kangaroo featured in the book, *Winnie-the-Pooh* she refused to answer to anything but Roo. She had decided that if her sister, Winnie, herself christened as Martha Winifred, named after my other grandma, got to be a Pooh, she could be a Roo. She dubbed me as Tigger for a short while, openly pleading with our parents to move to the Hundred Acre Wood. We called her Roo to appease her, thinking she would soon let go of it, but she didn't. We decided little Marguerite Ann had embraced the same tenacious spirit as her namesake and she would be called Roo if we wanted any response from her.

Roo was a little actress and talked nonstop, whether you were listening to her or not, mimicking conversations overheard from my mom's lengthy phone calls with friends or from viewing TV commercials, complete with spot-on voice imitations. My Dad sang bass for a barbershop quartet, and we would all crack up when Roo imitated his rendition of *Goodbye My Coney Island Baby,* her little lips pursed as she tried to sing as low as her six-year-old voice would allow, chin nearly touching her chest. She was constantly in motion, getting into cupboards and closets, using anything she found as props for her world of make-believe.

Winnie, on the other hand, quietly observed people. When she spoke, we usually stopped to listen since we didn't hear her voice that much. Roo and Winnie were at opposite ends of the talking spectrum. I suppose Roo decided Winnie wasn't using all of her own conversational space, so she would claim Winnie's non-spoken minutes as her own.

Winnie, like every other teenage girl her age, became absorbed in the world of soap operas for most of the day. In 1970, we only had ten TV channels, so soap operas or game shows ruled the screen from morning until late afternoon. If it weren't for commercial breaks, she would not have realized one day, that Roo was in the bathroom giving Skip a bubble bath, much to his dismay. Roo had poured a whole bottle of *Mr. Bubbles* into the old claw foot tub, and it was billowing with bubbles. Skip was lost somewhere inside.

Roo's commercial to Skip about the amazing benefits of using *Mr. Bubble,* was falling on the deaf ears of the impatient dog. "Hey kids, heard about the new bubbly way to take a bath?" Roo asked a droopy eared, Skip, "with

Mr. Bubble!" she squealed, in a perfect Shirley Temple imitation. "He's got a bubbly face and a bubbly nose, Mr. Bubble! He'll bubble you clean and soften your skin, Mr. Bubble! He'll bubble your nose," her nose rubbed Skip's nose, "and bubble your chin," she poked his chin with a finger full of bubbles, "it's so much fun when you hop in! Mis-ter Bubble!"

By the time Winnie popped her head inside the bathroom door, Skip had one paw out of the tub and was working on the second paw. I'm sure he was hoping by some miracle, to be set free by Winnie before disappearing forever into the bubble abyss. Roo had trimmed Skip's hair, which was all over the bathroom floor, and he now looked like a scrawny lion that had been to a bad hairdresser.

"Are you mad, Winnie?" Roo said instantaneously as she bolted upright to face the door before Winnie even uttered a word.

"Roo," Winnie let out a grimacing sigh, "what have you done?"

Winnie took Skip outside to rinse him with the hose and helped Roo clean up her mess without raising her voice or uttering one swear word. Winnie had the patience of a saint. Had it been me who found Roo, the story may have ended differently.

Winnie knew I wouldn't be anywhere near our house for most of the day. Jilly and I practically lived at Memorial Park during the summer. High School kids taught baton, cheer leading, and arts & crafts classes, which the city provided for free to all children twelve and under. We would go from class to class until lunch time and then home for lunch, via our bikes. The pinnacle of our summer was performing one of our routines in the Kiddies' Parade during the Last Chance Stampede & Fair Week in July.

Jilly's oldest sister, Jane, taught classes at the park. She decided that this year, it would be a good idea to teach a ballet class.

"Hey, cats," she always said cool things like that; no wonder my brother spent so much time at her house. "You should take my ballet class that I'm teaching at the park, otherwise they are going to cancel it, because no one has signed up for it." Jilly looked up to find a cloud to study, and I shuffled my foot at a patch of dirt in the grass, trying to avoid eye contact.

Jilly finally broke the silence, "You're kidding, right? Who wants to do ballet? Not us! We aren't the ballet type," which, even Jane knew was true. Jean cut-offs, t-shirts, holey tennis shoes, bubblegum chewing, and skinned knees was our daily wear. Truth be told, I probably hadn't put a comb through my pixie haircut since Sunday, when it was my turn to take a bath.

I think Jane was secretly thinking she was Professor Henry Higgins, and we were her Eliza Doolittles from *My Fair Lady,* and she would teach us to become proper ladies before the summer was over. "C'mon, Jilly, it will be fun! I promise you cats will dig it."

Jilly and Jane argued back and forth, until finally, Jilly's mom got involved, and decided Jilly needed more cultural experiences in her life, and she would most definitely be taking the ballet class. Of course, I would be dragged into the cultural experience, as well.

We showed up for Jane's class the next morning, along with Davy, a park regular. Davy had just completed fourth grade, but was so tiny, people often mistook him for being a six or seven-year-old. His wafer-thin face was dominated by black horn-rimmed glasses. He had a nervous tick that caused him to constantly shake his long blonde bangs out of his eyes or swipe them with his hand. Davy lived with his grandma across the street from the park, in an old apartment that had once been a seedy drive-up motel. Now it was a seedy apartment building.

When he was in first grade, Davy came home from school one afternoon and found his grandma lying on the kitchen floor. The little six-year-old thought she was dead, but it turned out to be a debilitating stroke. Authorities had no idea that six-year-old Davy continued to live at her house while his grandma recuperated in the hospital for three weeks. It was then that Davy learned the art of dumpster diving and stealing food from the local grocery store.

When his grandma finally returned home, her right hand denied her brain's orders to do simple tasks, while the right leg triggered a limp like Igor of the Frankenstein movies. Davy had been fending for himself all that time, and after her stroke, he would have to fend for his grandma as well.

Memorial Park was Davy's home away from home. He participated in every class that was offered. Davy greeted the park workers whose sleepy eyes squinted with the emerging sun, and was there to help turn off sprinklers for the night, gladly accepting any uneaten portions of their sack lunches.

The ballet class was held in the warming house at

Memorial Park, and the warming house was just that, a little hut used to warm up on cold winter days when the small sandlot was flooded to become an ice-skating rink. Rink attendants sold hot chocolate and candy inside the hut, and piped music onto the rink using a record player set near the microphone. Bright lights illuminating the little rink created a magical atmosphere. Jilly and I especially loved night skating, when the ice would be dominated by kids our age, and of course, the junior high crowd. We would spend the whole session screaming and laughing as we chased after boys trying to retrieve our waist-length stocking caps.

But on this hot summer day, we lined up at the vacant candy counter in the warming house to use as a ballet bar, skinned knees and all. "Stand up straight, eyes ahead, chin up, heels together, toes pointed out!" I swear Jane sounded like she had an English accent as she barked out orders.

Jilly noticed it, too. "Why are you talking like that?" Jilly frowned, "if you are trying to sound like Professor Higgins, you sound more like Flip Wilson doing his *Geraldine Jones'* bit on *Laugh-In*."

Davy apparently thought that comment was hilarious and over-enthusiastically fell down laughing on the wooden skate- nicked floor. "Geraldine Jones! Geraldine Jones! *What you see is what you get!*" he mimicked Flip Wilson's sassy voice as Geraldine Jones.

Flip Wilson was a comedian who guest starred on a weekly comedy show called, *Laugh-In*. My parents got a real kick out of seeing him dress up like a lady named Geraldine Jones. She had a boyfriend named Killer, only Flip pronounced it, *Killa*. Flip Wilson had some meat on his bones, so when he tried to walk in high heel shoes it was hilarious.

"C'mon man, quit fooling around and get back by the bar!" Jane insisted. Davy stood up and flipped his bangs out of his eyes with a toss of his head. He got back in line, smiling from ear to ear. "Now, first position, toes out, back straight, and slowly bend your knees. That is a plie'" she explained.

We all bent down awkwardly, tongues sticking out, feeling like we would topple over with one little nudge. "Backs straight! Now try it again."

Jane stopped abruptly with her hands on her hips and peered at Jilly, for what seemed like an eternity. She bent close to Jilly and sniffed twice, eyes narrowing and finally, "Are you chewing gum?" Jane asked, as though it was the worst thing she had ever witnessed in her life, her English accent at its finest. "Jilly, are you chewing gum?" she blinked as she stared three inches away from Jilly's face. Jane held out her hand and told Jilly to spit it out. I quickly stuck my wad onto the roof of my mouth, as Jilly spit the gum into Jane's hand. The dense mass made a thud as it landed at the bottom of the empty metal garbage can. Jane wiped the juice on her leg, which created a pink stain that formed the shape of the African continent on her white leotard.

"Plie' one, and two, and three," she continued.

It was about then that Davy's Van de Camp's pork and beans dinner from the night before started taking effect. At first, it appeared I was the only one who could hear him muttering, "Oh, man... oh geez... uh oh..." I turned halfway around and saw his furrowed brow with beads of sweat forming on his upper lip. He shook his head in a quivering quickness and motioned his eyes toward the front, wanting me to turn around so he did not draw attention to himself and have Jane turn her focus on him instead of Jilly.

But, in the next split second, he let his stored-up gas explosion loose on the fifth plie' which stopped Jane dead in her tracks. She pinched the bridge of her nose and closed her eyes, trying to contain her frustration. Finally, she looked to the ceiling and took a deep breath, probably hoping for Scotty to beam her up and teleport her back to Normal Town.

I turned to see Davy wide-eyed beneath his shaggy bangs, a teeth-revealing grin had spread across his face. I met Jilly's eyes and we both turned to study Davy. Suddenly, all three of us burst out laughing, and one by one dropped on the floor of the warming house, laughing so hard tears rolled out of our eyes.

The more Davy laughed the more bean explosions fired with each laugh. Davy clutched his stomach a smiling grimace on his face and fired away two plates full of the effects of his pork and bean dinner. "*The devil made me do it! The devil made me do it!*" he squealed in his best high-pitched Flip Wilson imitation of Geraldine Jones.

The students in the arts and crafts class heard the commotion and began to laugh at the spectacle across the room, all but forgetting their finger paint masterpieces laying haphazardly on the table. Chaos was in full throttle in the little warming house.

Jane flipped her long brown hair behind her shoulders and crossed her arms. She stood with her mouth open, eyebrows raised, eyes not quite registering what she was seeing and unsure how she had lost control of the situation. There was nothing she could do, and she knew it. As she watched Davy roll around on the floor and scanned the totally out of control room, her perfect white teeth began to emerge as Davy let go of each unintended explosion. Jane and the rest of the warming house shook with laughter.

That was our first and last cultural experience with ballet, and Jane decided that her ballet class just wasn't meant to be.

CHAPTER 4

Riding bikes provided an up close and personal view of the cracks and crevices of our neighborhood. We knew that Mr. Magoo's yard had the best rhubarb, Fay's crabapple trees were the sweetest in September, and if we walked past Mr. and Mrs. Hill's house early on Saturday mornings, we would be greeted with the best chocolate chip cookies on the block.

Jilly and I would sit on the Hill's front porch eating our cookies and watch with wonder as Mr. Hill, who was blind, mow his lawn with precision. Every blade of grass was perfectly manicured, not a dandelion on the premises. When he turned off the mower and we said hello, he knew exactly who we were. Once we tried to disguise our voices, but he laughed, and still knew exactly who was talking to him. He and Mrs. Hill never got angry if we happened to cut across their corner lot, either. They were like grandparents to all the kids on the block.

Mr. Docker, on the other hand, was quick to yell if we stepped one toe in his pristine yard. It was difficult to resist his four-foot-high wire fence, braced with two by fours that were perfect for practicing our balance beam skills. He absolutely blew a gasket when he saw us perched on the whitewashed beam as the furious *tap, tap, tap* with his knuckle on the kitchen window shooed us away. With the frantic rapping, we were sure the glass would one day break, and the pointy shards would be his demise.

Mrs. Peters lived directly across the street from my house. She sat near her window every day watching our antics as though we were a live TV sitcom. Rolling down the hill on my front lawn, skateboarding up and down the sidewalk, practicing cartwheel after cartwheel, and playing games of 500 and more, produced constant squeals and laughter, and squabbles over who won. It was quite an entertaining spectacle, and all presented free of charge for the lonely little woman across the street.

We were watchful when Mrs. Peters stepped outside to sweep her sidewalks, or when she would pretend to study her flowerbeds, making sideways glances to spy on us from across the street. Every so often, she would wave a dollar bill, and yell in her shaky, high pitched screech, "You kids! You kids! Come get this for The Creamery!"

The Creamery was a small ice cream shop that was just a short walk from our house. Its formal name was The Ice Cream Parlor, but she always referred to it as The Creamery. Mrs. Peters would treat us to ice cream cones, and in return, we would pick up some milk or other dairy items that she needed. Jilly and I would argue over which one of us would have to approach Mrs. Peters to get the money. She didn't exactly ask us to take the money, but more likely demanded we come and get it. We were excited that she was treating us to an ice cream cone, but a little unnerved at the thought of getting close enough to grab the money, so she could take a whack at us with her broom.

However, Mrs. Peters was not waving a dollar bill today. She was sitting on her porch swing, with no visible reaction to our noisy arrival. Jilly nudged me, "I wonder what's wrong with her?" She seemed to be asleep, her head leaned against the stucco wall behind her. A yellow paper fluttered from her grasp to the porch floor. I wondered what was on it, we both did, but neither of us was brave enough to approach her. Her broom was laying haphazardly on the sidewalk in front of her house, so out of place from her tidy habits.

For a split second, I thought she was dead until she used the back of her hand to wipe both eyes and turned her head toward my house. She noticed Jilly and me standing there and stood to shuffle through her screen door, leaving the broom in the middle of her sidewalk and the paper laying on her front porch. We looked at each other and shrugged. I turned to study Mrs. Peters' house, feeling uneasy, but still afraid to approach her, to see if she was okay. I had never had a real conversation with her.

"I'll be back at 1:45 to go to our softball game," Jilly whispered, eyes still on the lookout for Mrs. Peters as she turned and rode off up the street.

I sat down on my front porch step and eyed Mrs. Peters' empty porch swing and waited for her to take her place inside the house, on her radiator by the front window, but she never did. It was a well-known fact she was a cranky old lady, but the only way to describe the look on her face this day, was a word that Mrs. Holt had used once: woeful.

I could hear our TV on inside. Upon opening our screen door, Nurse Audrey March Baldwin from *General Hospital* was sobbing as she revealed to everyone that she was mistaken about being with child. I wondered what Dr. Tom Baldwin would think when he found out, since he had married her to make things right. Things were all a flutter at *General Hospital* as I fixed a bologna sandwich for lunch.

Winnie's eyes glistened, as she sat riveted to Audrey's speech. Six-year-old, Roo, had one of my mom's nurse's caps on her head and was listening to Winnie's heart with her doctor kit's stethoscope. Winnie had a bandage wrapped around her head and a sling on her arm.

"I'm sorry, miss," Roo shook her head, "your heart has stopped beating. Hmmm… yes, you are dead as a doorknob. Here is some medicine to bring you back to life," and she filled a spoon full of Hawaiian Punch and put it into Winnie's mouth. Winnie swallowed without even flinching away from Audrey's devastating news.

I sat down to see if Dr. Tom would find out about Audrey, and secretly wished he would tell her to go take a hike. She was a jerk to everyone in Port Charles, but each time Dr. Tom came around, Audrey poured on the charm. Dr. Tom was in surgery during Audrey's dramatic scene, so he wouldn't find out today. I finished my bologna sandwich and looked for my softball mitt.

After lunch, Jilly and I rode our stingrays to the Memorial Park sandlot for our first softball game of the summer. Our team was about to warm up, and we ran to join them on the field. Games were played in the afternoon, so there really weren't any parents or fans watching us play, but we could always count on Davy to be there and cheer us on, since he didn't have anything else better to do.

The girls on my softball team were mostly neighborhood kids and we would continue to be friends throughout my life. We were a scrappy crew and tenacity flowed like water. We lived for the game and would never give up until the ump officially declared the game to be over.

Mo at center field could throw a bullseye all the way from center field to the catcher's mitt, quite a feat for an eleven-year-old. She was smart and most likely to be a brain surgeon when she grew up.

Flanking her at left field was Tara, whose long brown curly ponytail was never without a ribbon, but who had as much grit and determination as the rest of us. Mary Carol at rover, whose wavy blonde hair never had a ribbon and blew freely in the breeze. Even though softball wasn't her strong suit, her rocket scientist mind hatched up some far-fetched schemes and plans during our lifetime that provided memories that made parents wince.

Mary Elizabeth played right field. I would often look her way as I took the mound, to see her desperately motioning for me to keep the pitch inside. She was the only person on our team, who didn't want the ball to come her way. Her black bangs grazed just above the lids of her big green eyes; eyes that showed great fear as hand and mitt clasped together in prayer. I would crack up, she was so hysterical, and didn't even know it.

Playing shortstop was Sooner, she could stop a ball cold, and was usually covered in dirt at the end of games because of her diving catches and will to win every game. She was always there when you needed her, on or off the field.

Cal played second and was the most consistent at hitting and catching. Her dad being a high school coach, she was the one on our team who had technique. Sid, on third, held an important position, because she was another one who kept me laughing. Don't get me wrong, she could stop a grounder like no one's business, whether it was with her mitt, or her body. She also ran the bases like Speedy Gonzales.

Jilly on first, to make the seemingly out of reach catches by stretching her long legs. Trixie as catcher, even though she closed her eyes when we threw her the ball, she added the spunk to our team and provided the smack talk to the batters. Me at pitcher, because somehow, I could get the ball to land over the plate into Trixie's mitt.

As far as uniforms, there weren't any. Boys who played baseball in our town were decked out in matching uniforms, complete with cleats, bat bags, and a bleacher full of fans. Our girls' softball team wore whatever we put on that morning, along with sneakers, that didn't have the traction to keep us from slipping and sliding on the all dirt field. It was rare to see any parents at our games since all games were played during the day, and most of our parents were working.

Our coach was a senior in high school and volunteered for the position so she could add community service to her college resume. She tried hard, and did have the use of her dad's truck, so those qualifications made her a good candidate for the position. She knew most of the rules for softball, but we had to fill her in on those she didn't understand, like the tricky infield fly rule and the fact that you could stay in the batter's box for as many foul balls as you could hit.

Having the truck was an important qualification, so if we won a game, the team could pile in the back and head to A&W for celebratory root beers. There was nothing like the cold sweet taste of a frosty mug of root beer after playing softball in the 90-degree Montana sun.

We finished warming up, and three teenage umpires sauntered on to the field a minute before game time. They were local kids hired by the City of Helena, who did not let their youthfulness take any crap from coaches or players.

Lawn chair in hand, one of the umps took her place on the third base line. Sleeves rolled up to her shoulders to avoid a farmer's tan, she stretched out in the lawn chair, face to the sun, as though she were enjoying a lazy afternoon by the city pool. Flip flops kicked aside; all her calls would be made from the comfort of her lawn chair. If permissible, she would have welcomed a tropical drink complete with a little umbrella to sip on while she marked hits and runs in the scorebook. For now, the cooler of Bergie Beer waiting for her in the back seat of her 1961 Ford Galaxy Convertible would have to suffice.

The tall intimidating high schooler took her place behind the plate. She called 'em as she saw 'em, and there was no arguing with her. However, her generous strike zone worked to my advantage as a pitcher. She didn't want the game to drag on and on, like they sometimes did, so batters up, had to basically swing at any ball that was within range of their bat, whether it was way above their head or a chip shot barely skimming home plate.

The newbie ump had quite possibly never played softball in her life. Her mother was the mayor of our town, so her Barbie doll daughter was granted the umpiring position because the park and recreation manager wanted to keep his job. We watched this Annette Funicello with her huge white sunglasses take her place in the outfield wondering if Frankie Avalon and the gang would be following behind her. Her bright pink pedal pushers matched a floppy hat that could have been a contender at an Easter parade or the Kentucky Derby. Her umping technique for calling close plays at second was to look at the third base ump for the call, and then yell, "OUT!" or "SAFE!" accordingly. Once she yelled, "Out!" and looked to the lawn chair ump, who was shaking her head, and yelled, "No, wait, I mean safe! Yes, definitely safe!"

Our coach only rolled her eyes, because arguing over the call would be of no use. The home plate umpire had aspirations for law school and practiced her court room arguments on young flustered high school coaches. The last time our coach tried to protest a call, the ump yelled, "Objection!" and pointed at her to take her place on the clump of grass next to the fence that we used as a "dugout," since girls' softball didn't have dugouts, or even benches to sit on when we weren't in the field.

The game was anything but a barn burner. The plate umpire had to pause the game during the first inning, to give the opposing pitcher a mini pitching lesson. "For the love of god…" she muttered as she headed to the mound. The pitcher could not, for the life of her, get the ball anywhere near the range of our bats. The score was 18-0, no outs, in the top of the first inning, and the ump was pissed! She did not want this game to go past her required eight hour working day.

41

When we finally made it to the second inning, the third base ump looked at the clock hanging on the warming house, and noticed it was quitting time, and yelled, "Game over!" We all stared at her because it was only the top of the second inning. But she folded up her lawn chair and spit out the remaining sunflower seeds that had been stored in her cheek. The other two umps concurred and disappeared into the warming house.

"Okay then," our coach raised her eyebrows, "I, uh, guess we won. Let's go get those root beers." And with that, we cheered and ran off the field, leaving the other team, mouths agape, still standing on the field.

CHAPTER 5

That evening, my dad was watching Walter Cronkite's report on the Vietnam War, which had been going on for my lifetime. It had been on the news since the day I was born, and troops wouldn't start coming home for another five years.

The graphic pictures of dead and injured soldiers plastered newspapers, magazines, and newscasts and there was no way to avoid seeing it, unless you lived in the woods as a hermit. It appeared the world was imploding and seeing it on TV every night made it too real.

People were on edge and college students were protesting the Vietnam War on campuses all over the United States. One of the worst protests was at Kent State University in Ohio. Four student protesters were killed when things got out of hand.

The photo of one student who had been shot dead was plastered on the cover of *Life* magazine. I'll never forget the image of a girl kneeling next to a lifeless victim, one arm raised helplessly, the other hand grasping a bystander, in a desperate plea for him to do something. Her mouth poised as if she was screaming, "Why?" I could hear her agonizing scream each time I passed by the magazine laying nonchalantly on our coffee table.

The night prior, there had been violent clashes in downtown Kent between students and the police. Bottles were thrown at police cars and bonfires lit in the streets causing traffic to stop. The Kent mayor declared a state of emergency and the Ohio National Guard was called in to help calm the tensions. By that time, protesters had already set fire to the ROTC building, and even worse, protestors reportedly had clashed with the firefighters who were attempting to put out the fire.

The next morning, there were rumors about threats made against businesses in Kent as well as to buildings on the campus and tensions were high. Protestors were ordered to disperse but refused and began throwing rocks and shouting at the Guardsmen. The Guardsmen forced the protestors up a nearby hill and into a football practice field that was enclosed with fencing, which caused the Guardsmen to be caught amongst the angry mob. The shouting and thrown rocks continued as the Guardsmen retreated up the hill, concerned for their own safety. Witnesses to the event say they suddenly turned and fired their rifles into the air, and some fired directly into the crowd of protestors. Four student protesters lay dead after the 13-seconds of shots being fired.

That unforgettable moment in Kent State's history became a symbol for the disharmony of the public's opinion of the Vietnam War.

As much as I hated the war, I despised the hateful

protestors who screamed obscenities and hurled rocks at troops who were only trying to protect the town. Their violence made me uneasy. My brothers, Duke and Jack, would both be heading to basic training soon to become members of Montana's National Guard and I couldn't stand the thought of one of them, or my dad for that matter, ending up on Walter Cronkite's news cast because they were trying to keep peace in our state.

However, I was thankful that they would serve the state of Montana but would not be drafted and sent to Vietnam by the United States Army. Even though neither one could resist a punch to my arm as I walked by them or hold back a threat to give me a knuckle sandwich, I would never wish to see them in harm's way.

There were three other girls in this family, but I was prime target for my brothers' teenage angst, most likely because my fiery reactions were highly entertaining to them. I could never let things be when they walked by and punched my arm or extend an elbow jab at the dinner table. My retaliations would take place a few hours later when they weren't expecting it. Typically, as luck would have it, my mom would get wind of my revenge and blame me for the whole thing. I swear, Duke and Jack never got in trouble, and they always started it, which could have been hours, days, or weeks prior.

There was a time when my mom thought Jack was destined for the priesthood. He had been an altar boy in his younger years and seemed to have some kind of saintly presence, according to my mom and her sister, Patricia, who had been devout Catholics all their lives. I had to admit, he was super nice, when he wasn't punching my arm. I thought he would be a cool priest because of his shoulder length hair and Foo Manchu mustache that he grew after graduating from high school, which gave him a strong resemblance to the picture of Jesus, Mom had hanging in her bedroom.

I think my mom finally realized that the priesthood wasn't his calling when my parents got wind of some unpriestly-like behavior, at the end of his senior year in high school.

Jack had been at the Senior Kegger, a rite of passage for the graduating students of Helena High School. That year, it was held on the other side of McDonald Pass, in a wooded area. The sheriff in Deer Lodge County got wind of it, and he didn't take too kindly to underage drinkers, so he and his deputies swarmed in like a Dragnet swat team. Jack and his friends spent the next four hours hiding in the mountains, from the cops, and trying to figure out how to bail the rest of their gang out of the Deer Lodge jail.

Duke, on the other hand, may or may not have been seminary material, but nevertheless, a golden child. He had been captain of the football and basketball teams and played Legion baseball in the summer. He managed to get good grades and went to Boys' State, an honor bestowed on only the best and brightest students in the class.

Duke's sun-bleached bangs swooped low on his forehead framing a perfectly white toothed smile, which drew the attention of giggling girls. His tanned frame looked to be more of a surfer riding the waves near a California beach town, rather than a kid living in the mountains of Montana. To top that off, he dated Jilly's sister, Jane, who was a cheerleader, and the prettiest girl in the school. With all of that going for him, we knew he was destined for greatness.

But then Duke decided to enroll for college at the University of Montana in Missoula. Missoula was way ahead of its time and known for its diverse and eclectic student body, even though it was within a state known for horses and conservative cowboys.

My dad referred to the U of M as "Hippie-ville." Dad believed the U of M had an over-abundance of long-haired hippies and was sure they came straight from Woodstock in their multicolored buses, to brainwash gullible Montana kids into believing their liberal baloney about peace and love. Don't get me wrong, my dad liked peace, and he liked love, but he liked my brother getting a job more.

After Duke had entered college, my parents were surprised to find out that the golden child would come to Helena on weekends, to party with friends, not even calling home or staying at our house. They became aware of his weekend trips one Sunday afternoon, when my dad was driving to State Nursery on Highway 12, with Roo. Of course, the observant Roo, noticed a hitchhiker thumbing for a ride to Missoula, and out of curiosity inquired, "Dad, why is Duke standing on the highway?" And that was the moment they realized the golden child didn't quite have the shimmering glow of perfection that had followed him throughout his childhood and teenage years.

Mrs. Peters' grandson, Jesse, was just a few years older than Duke, and was serving a tour in Vietnam. Jesse didn't have a mother in his life, she had run off, right after he was born, and they had not heard from her since. Jesse's dad, the Peters' only son, had been killed in the Korean War, and Mr. and Mrs. Peters had raised Jesse as a son ever since he was four years old.

In 1968, Jesse's name was called up for the draft. I had watched him say goodbye to his grandparents as he left for basic training, one snowy morning, the day after Christmas.

A motor idling on the street in front of our house woke me. I tiptoed over to the window and peeked to see who was parked outside. Huge snowflakes drifted down amid the glow of the streetlights, creating a winter wonderland. Mr. and Mrs. Peters were standing on their front porch with Jesse, who had a duffle bag at his feet. Tree branches bowed from the weight of the fresh blanket of snow, and created a frame around the three of them, as they stood on the porch of the little brick house. The antique streetlights, straight out of a Dickens' novel, provided a warm yellow glow to the house and the sparkling snow falling all around them. The scene before me looked to be a setting in one of my snow-globes, but no snow-globe depicted a family saying goodbye to a soldier who was leaving home to fight a war in Vietnam.

Mrs. Peters grasped Jesse's hands and placed what looked like rosary beads inside them and sealed them with a kiss. Her cheek rested on his clasped hands, not wanting to let go.

I swallowed hard thinking about her only son who was killed in the Korean War, it must have been fresh in her mind. That had been Jesse's dad. When she finally let go, Mr. Peters went to shake Jesse's hand, but Jesse pulled him close and hugged his grandfather, both giving each other solid pats on the back. Jesse would have no way of knowing at that time, but one month after that embrace, his grandfather would be dead from a heart attack.

Mrs. Peters had lived alone in the little house across the street ever since her husband's death. Jesse did not make it home for his grandfather's funeral. That was over a year ago.

That night as I went to bed, I wondered what was written on the paper lying on Mrs. Peters' front porch and thought that maybe it had something to do with her grandson, Jesse.

CHAPTER 6

After dinner, Jilly and I met our gang of friends from school on the Cathedral lawn. We liked playing on the steep grassy hill. Although the priests may have thought differently, the neighborhood kids found it to be the perfect hill for rolling down or playing King of the Mountain. In the wintertime, it was the best sledding hill because it had a hump right in the middle. When your sled hit it at maximum speed, you would bypass the second hump and not touch down until you hit the icy parking lot, blasting your sled straight into the hard brick wall of Bishop Gilmore School on the other side of the lot.

We divided up into two teams to play Kick the Can, and my team hid first. I ran and kicked the can and we all scattered. The other team had to count to one hundred before they came looking for us to capture as prisoners. We decided that hiding inside the Cathedral was acceptable, but the altar area was off limits, that would have been sacrilegious.

I raced to the front entrance of the church taking the steps two by two and opened the huge door. Out of habit, I blessed myself with holy water from the marble font and ran toward a marble pillar near the front of the church. My footsteps echoed loudly, and I realized mine were the only footsteps inside the church; everyone else must have hid outside. I got down on my hands and knees and crawled under one of the pews near a pillar, trying to quiet my breathing so I wouldn't give myself away.

The cloudy evening cooled the air and made it darker than usual inside the church, and I was getting a little creeped out, because it appeared that I was the only one hiding in there. I started to hope someone from the other team would at least come in to look for me, so I would not be all alone.

As I crouched under the pew, I could see a partial view of one of the stained-glass windows that told the story of Jesus' life. Jesus was carrying the heavy wooden cross as the angry Roman soldiers looked on. Studying the window, I wondered if deep down, the soldiers felt sorry for Jesus, but were too afraid to admit it, for fear of being forced to carry their own wooden crosses down the same path.

Suddenly, I heard a soft murmur and crouched lower, waiting to see which person on the other team had come inside to search for prisoners. I waited several minutes, wondering why they hadn't come down the aisle looking for me.

I decided to peek and see who had come in. It was even darker now as I ducked under pews to look at the person's feet. The feet I saw were wearing a large size pair of worn-out boots, too big for any of my friends. I swallowed, wondering who was sitting in the church pew. My heart began to beat double time and I hoped he couldn't hear my heavy breathing. I did not see him when I entered the church, so I wondered how he came to be in the pew.

I crawled around the marble pillar to get a better look and saw an old man sitting in the pew. His elbows rested on his knees; forehead bowed on his tightly clasped hands. He looked like he had the world on his shoulders, and reminded me of Enstrom's painting, *Grace,* that Jilly had on her kitchen wall. I could hear bits and pieces of the *Lord's Prayer* in his whisper.

I had a sudden urge to ask him if he was okay but thought better of it. My mom would have had a spaz attack if she knew I was playing hide and seek in the Cathedral, let alone addressing a complete stranger. As I stared from behind the pillar, I knew this was an invasion of a very personal moment, yet I could not look away.

I heard my friends screaming outside, no doubt, someone was charging to home base to kick the can and free my teammates from their prison. I turned around to crawl toward the back of the church, but my shoelace became caught in the kneeler, and I fell on the wooden edges of it with a loud echoing thud. "Dang it," I breathed, and grabbed my aching knee wincing in pain. I tried to stand up, but my lace was still caught. I worried the stranger had heard my clumsy fall.

I was desperately yanking on my shoe, trying to free it from the kneeler, when a shadow crossed over my foot, instantly giving me the chills. I felt all the blood drain from my face and froze in place. My eyes moved toward the shadow and I spotted the worn-out boots and followed a dirty pant leg up to the face of the stranger. We locked eyes. Dark circles contrasted the deep blue color. I realized, then that the eyes weren't old, just tired.

He put both hands up as though to calm my fear, and one finger pointed to my shoelace that was hooked on the hinge, and I reached down and untangled it.

I checked my throbbing knee and smoothed a torn pant leg over my waffle stomper. "Thank y…," I said as I turned to face him, but he was gone. I stood and looked up and down the aisle, but he was nowhere in sight. "Where did he go?" I wondered aloud. I darted down the aisle to see if I could get a glimpse of him, but he had vanished, by the time I pushed open the large church door.

"That was weird," I muttered to myself, and reached down to assess my tender knee, and fingered my torn jeans. "Dang, how am I going to explain my ripped pant leg to my mom? Ugh!" I wasn't good at lying, my mom could see right through me. "Mom and Dad will have a conniption fit if they find out I've been playing Kick the Can inside the Cathedral," I thought.

I imagined my mom on the phone the next morning telling my aunt Patricia all about my scandalous behavior. "Oh, my Lord, Patricia, that child has pushed the limits this time. Can you imagine? Playing hide and seek *inside the Cathedral*, of all places! What will Father Oblinger say?"

"Glory be to God, Betty! What on Earth got into her?" my aunt would be aghast. I could picture the kitchen wall phone, with the six-foot cord stretched inside the basement door as they discussed my lack of common sense. That would be a good two-hour phone conversation.

When I got outside, I scanned the lawn for the

stranger, but he had disappeared into thin air. I was jolted back to my senses when I suddenly heard voices approaching and hurriedly jumped into a nearby window well.

"I ain't goin' back there," a voice snarled, "they ain't gonna find me." I heard him slide to a sitting position, very near the window well. I tried to make myself as small as possible.

"Damn, he did a number on you this time," another boy remarked, "what the hell? Man, your eye, it don't look too good."

The other boy laughed bitterly, "I'm getting' out of this town."

I recognized the voice of Harvey Dill. I decided the second voice must have been his twelve-year-old cousin, Rooster Dill, who didn't seem to have the same mean streak as Harvey, just a weird name. I knew exactly who had done the number on Harvey though, it was his dad. As much as I couldn't stand Harvey, I hated his dad, more.

The smoke from their cigarettes wafted into the window well where I was still hiding. I heard one of them spit several times, then, "Shit, my tooth! My damn tooth! Is that my tooth?" Harvey asked Rooster.

"Oh, man, you look like a jack o' lantern, dude," Rooster answered, and I pictured him wincing as he examined the gaping hole that once held Harvey's missing yellow tooth. "C'mon, we should go to my house while my parents are still at the Red Meadow. You better hide out for a while, until your old man cools down."

As they stood to leave, Rooster grabbed on to a metal bar that surrounded the window well to hoist himself up. I winced at his surprise when he suddenly noticed me crouched below.

"Who 'er you?" he squinted at me.

Harvey looked over the railing to investigate and saw me stand up at the far side of the well. "Lundberg!" he shouted my last name, "what the hell are you doing down there? Are you spying on us?" he accused.

"No! No, I uh..." I stammered, trying to find the words, "I was just playing Kick the Can, and..."

Suddenly, the man from the church appeared from nowhere, "Hey" his voice was barely audible, "you Harvey? Someone's looking for you, '58 Dodge."

Harvey's face blanched white as he swallowed a golf ball down his throat. He and Rooster's wide eyes blinked in disbelief. Harvey chewed on a dirty thumbnail and spit out a shard, or whatever else was hiding under it. They were afraid, there was no doubt about that.

"Lundberg, you'd better not say one word," he gritted his teeth and pointed down at me, "so help me god, I will find you and Gardner, and mess you up so bad, you won't know up from down." His mouth formed a thin line, his breath forced out of his nose like a rabid dog, ready to tear apart anything in its path. He then spit at me, but it dribbled down his chin because of the missing tooth. Wiping his bloody mouth with back of his arm, his red eyes threw daggers at me. I swallowed my own golf ball.

"Let's go!" Rooster urged, and they both took off running away from the church. Harvey turned and pointed

55

a grimy finger at me one more time, to solidify his threat.

I climbed up out of the window well and sat on the grass, not sure if my teeth were chattering from the cool night air, or fear. I had no idea where the strange guy had gone, but I didn't want to hang around to find out. Thankfully, I heard someone yell, "Ollie, ollie, oxen free!" Which meant the game was over. I got up and ran around to the far side of the church. As I rounded the corner, I breathed a sigh of relief when I saw the rest of the kids in the parking lot talking to Father Dolan.

Father Dolan had been a priest at the Cathedral for less than a year. He was young and had just been newly ordained. I guess being the greenhorn, he was the one who had to always check on our shenanigans when we were playing at the Cathedral.

I could hear him singing, "Jeremiah was a bullfrog…" It cracked me up that a priest would sing a song like that and not *Sons of God,* or *Ave Maria,* or something churchy like that. He didn't judge us for playing on church property either or try to run us off. I think he knew we respected the Cathedral and would never do anything to harm it.

Father Dolan held his hand out to give me five when I walked up, "Hey, Betts!" I was still reeling from Harvey's threat, and he must have sensed something was wrong. "Everything okay?" I gave his outstretched hand a five, and nodded, not wanting to say anything about dumb Harvey. He nodded back but hesitated as he studied my eyes before turning toward the rest of the group.

CHAPTER 7

Father Dolan had grown up in Helena, so the people of our parish knew his life story. He was quite mischievous as a child and had a reputation for getting into fights as he grew to be a teenager. As a result, the local police knew him well.

One night, he and some friends were laying chase on a group of boys from Butte, who were in town for a basketball game. Sean Dolan was riding in the back of a pickup truck as they went flying up Grizzly Gulch, ready for a rumble. The truck hit some loose gravel and started fish tailing. The driver lost control, and the truck, carrying Sean in its bed, flipped over several times. Sean was thrown thirty feet from the truck and slammed into the trunk of a Douglas Fir, where he slid down into some shrubs at its base. He was temporarily lost, which caused a frantic search by his friends who used the full moon as their only light source.

The boys from Butte slowed to a stop when they realized the truck that was pursuing them had lost control and rolled down an embankment. The boys looked at each other for a brief second thinking this was their chance to make a run for it, but their instincts were to get help. The driver flipped a u-turn and high-tailed it down the road to call for an ambulance at the nearest house. By the time they returned with the emergency crew, Sean Dolan's friends were mourning his death.

A police officer was the first responder to the scene and immediately began CPR. After an eternity, Sean's eyes began to flutter and blink their way open. He gasped, as his friends watched wide-eyed, hands holding on to their heads in disbelief, faces wet with relief. The Butte boys, only feet away, stood speechless, hearts pounding, the full moon reflecting shiny eyes.

Sean mumbled, "Not yet... not yet..." The onlookers froze, breathless, hands suspended mid-air so as not to miss a single syllable uttering from Sean's mouth. In the following weeks, they would come to understand that their mischievous friend would no longer be accompanying them to rumbles and summertime shenanigans.

Sean was taken to St. Peter's Hospital and had emergency surgery to repair a shattered hip, which would mean the use of a cane for the rest of his life.

Everyone, including Sean, believed it was a miracle that he had come out of that experience alive, but that would not be the only miracle of Sean Dolan. As he lay dead on the forest floor, he later told his family he had felt himself being lifted off the ground, hovering higher and higher above the commotion. He could see his friends and paramedics working to bring his body back to life. Sean recited specific conversations between the paramedics as he lay there lifeless while they pumped madly on his chest. He smiled when his buddy, Joey's eyes widened, as Sean asked him where his coveted Mickey Mantle rookie baseball card was that he had promised to give Sean if he would just wake up.

Sean spoke of an out of body experience and being transported to another dimension, maybe it was heaven? As he watched curiously at the commotion below him, a sudden brilliant white light enveloped his being, emoting a warmth, comparable to the protection a baby feels in its mother's arms. The loving presence carried him to the most beautifully peaceful place he had ever seen or felt. It embodied incredibly crisp colors that could not be described, they were colors he had never seen in his life. His head became saturated by a musical presence, unlike any voices or instruments he had ever heard that radiated love, extraordinary love. This encompassing love flowed from every single animate and inanimate object surrounding him. Such wonderment and joy, he did not want to speak by using his own dull voice, it would not be worthy of such transcendency. Sean Dolan did not want to leave and conveyed his feelings without speaking to the divine presence, which by then he decided was Jesus Christ.

As Sean neared the divine light, he first regarded a bright form which he believed to be his grandmother. Her smile exuded joy and Sean felt perfect in her presence. As if on a movie reel, he saw his five-year-old self at a family reunion in Rimini, which happened to be the last time he had seen his grandma before she passed away, the sad look in his mom's eyes at her 50th birthday party that Sean didn't attend because he had "better things to do," and then a fight that he had had with his brother, Patrick, over whose turn it was to use the car. But then he saw the smiles and laughter of Christmas mornings, trips to

Disneyland, picnics at the Little Blackfoot, his dad's laughter as he gave Sean his first driving lesson, and on and on through his entire seventeen years. It was a life review and Sean could see exactly how his presence and actions had affected each person that he had come into contact with during his earthly life.

When the reel was complete, his grandmother communicated that it was time to go back. "Not yet," Sean pled with her. "Not yet." But it was not his choice and the light began to recede in the distance, becoming the size of a pin head until he was slammed back into his body on the forest floor.

Sean Dolan had been resuscitated and would find his life on Earth taking a one hundred eighty-degree turn. Instead of serving time in the local jail, Father Sean Dolan would now serve time with the Lord.

His story had been featured in local and national newspapers and finally found its way to *The Merv Griffin Show,* where Sean Dolan described his experience to the world. I was only four or five at the time, but I remember hurrying through dinner, so we wouldn't miss seeing the most famous person to come out of our town on live TV, since Gary Cooper. Father Sean Dolan was famous, and the kids in our neighborhood relished that fact.

CHAPTER 8

The next morning, we had baton lessons at Memorial Park. Diane, our teacher, taught us a routine to the *Hawaii Five-0* theme song, which we would perform at the Kiddie's Parade during the Stampede Fair and Rodeo week, in July.

The Stampede Rodeo and Fair was the best time of the year. The traveling carnival would come to town and we would spend hours at the fairgrounds riding the Zipper, Tilt-a-Whirl, and Scrambler and eating funnel cakes and hot dogs on a stick. The barns would be filled with 4-H animals, food, and homemade crafts, and people would come from all over Lewis and Clark County to take part in the festivities.

My mom and Aunt Patricia typically fixed a huge picnic lunch of fried chicken, potato salad, pork & beans, watermelon, and for dessert, homemade blonde brownies. My parents and aunt and uncle would sit in lawn chairs enjoying the summer afternoon, watching the comings and goings of the eclectic people who seemed to come out of the woodwork for the fair.

Jilly and I dreamed of performing our baton routine at the Kiddie's Parade during the Stampede. We would learn parts of routines and go home and practice for hours in our back yards. After the lesson, we were practicing our routine in my backyard. The seventh time through the routine, Jilly held her hand up, "Shh," she turned her ear toward the street. We both heard the familiar ringing… "Sno-Cone Lady!" we yelled simultaneously.

We took the back steps two at a time and ran straight through the house and out the front door. Roo and Winnie automatically knew the urgency, and both jumped up from the couch. I did a double take at Winnie, noticing the sponge rollers hanging sporadically through her long thick hair and what appeared to be whip cream on her face. Roo was obviously giving Winnie the spa treatment today. Didn't matter though, the Sno-Cone Lady was top priority, whether you were a kindergartner or a soon to be high schooler in curlers with whip cream on your face.

The Sno-Cone Lady drove down our street once a day, and it seemed a sin to miss her visit. Her little golf cart putted around neighborhoods all summer long, ringing the bell to alert the kids. We would dig for change in seat cushions, pants pockets, the washing machine, anywhere nickels, dimes and pennies might lay unforgotten.

Last summer when I couldn't find a dime to buy a sno-cone. Jilly and I frantically picked ten apples from my tree to see if the Sno-Cone Lady would trade a delicious cherry sno-cone for ten green apples. She looked at our pleading eyes and gave in, "Those apples look delicious. You have a deal." We all knew the green color was a sign the apples weren't quite ripe, and their sourness would barely be tolerable to eat. I had dreams of becoming a Sno-Cone Lady when I was in high school, and I most definitely would return the favor someday, to some poor deserving little kid who was dying for a cherry sno-cone, on a hot summer day.

Jilly and I sat on my front lawn letting the flavored ice quench our dry throats. It was a perfect summer day. The smell of freshly mowed lawns mingled with whiffs of wet concrete sidewalks as sprinklers overshot intended grass targets. The ash trees lining the street were thick with leaves, creating a tunnel of green for drivers to enter.

The city of Helena employed high school kids to water the trees and mow the grass on the boulevard. Jilly and I sat and watched one of the workers make his way down the street.

As he neared the house Jilly studied him for a minute, tilting her head and frowning as though she was trying to solve a mystery. "What's your name?" she asked bluntly.

"Alvin."

"Do you go to high school?"

"Yep."

"Do you know my sister, Cate? Cate Gardner?"

He looked up from watering, "Maybe."

"How about her sister," she motioned to me. "Winnie Lundberg?"

"You're Winnie Lundberg's sister? Hmm…" He

looked at me and raised an eyebrow, "Is this your house?"

"Yeah," I answered trying to sound cool, but when I opened my mouth to answer, a piece of ice fell from my mouth onto my foot. Without taking my eyes from him, I used my other foot to wipe it off.

"Is Winnie home?" He looked at our house.

"Yeah, do you want me to get her?" Before he could answer I yelled, "Winnie! Winnie, come out here!"

Winnie opened the screen door still holding her blueberry sno-cone. Her hair was still in curlers and whip cream sadly dripping off her face. "Betts, geez, stop yell…" Her eyes grew wide when she noticed Alvin standing on our boulevard. Roo had added a maroon sweatband around Winnie's head, and a necklace made of macaroni noodles, which definitely complimented Winnie's exotic look. Her teeth and lips bore a faint shade of blue from the sno-cone.

"Hey, Winnie," Alvin grinned.

"Uh, hi, Alvin," she blushed, and touched the curlers in her hair, doing her best to straighten them, as if that would make a difference. "Um, I need to go inside, it was nice seeing you." She closed the screen door, obviously embarrassed, her eyes pierced daggers at me.

Alvin had a big smile on his face. I'm not sure if he was amused at Winnie's appearance or if he liked her. "Well, I need to get back to work. See you around," and he unhooked the hose from the water main and headed to the next dry section of boulevard.

Jilly and I looked at each other and laughed. "Did

you see his goofy smile? Geez Louise!" I rolled my eyes and shook my head.

"I don't think Winnie was too happy about you calling her outside when she looked like a mummy rising from the dead," Jilly laughed.

"I know. I probably shouldn't go in my house right now. Let's walk up to Central School."

As we neared Central, we ran past the old high school and raced to the swings on the playground. We both jumped on swings and began madly pumping our legs to see who could go the highest and jump off the farthest. The chains on the old swing set were extra-long so you could go way high up in the air. We were going higher and higher. This was going to be an epic jump since the playground teachers were not around to make us stop.

As I reached the highest point possible, I glanced over at the old high school. My eyes locked on a broken window thinking I had seen something move. I strained my neck to keep focused on the window, but it was hard to keep track of it when I was going back and forth, so I dragged my feet to slow down. My eyes were glued on the window, and once more I noticed the movement and stopped in a lurch.

"I'm Superwoman!" Jilly yelled and flew so far out of the swing, she rolled forward and landed with an "Oomph!"

When she realized I had stopped swinging, she turned her eyes toward the target of my focus. "Do you see that, Jilly? Something is moving inside the building," I whispered. We both froze, eyes not blinking. "Do you see someone looking out the window?"

Jilly was staring at the window. "The miner's ghost," she joked in a Dracula impersonation, but then her eyes grew wide, when she saw something move.

Jilly grabbed onto me and we stood there, cheek to cheek, hands balled in fists next to our faces. We spied another movement. "Holy crap," I whispered, "there is someone in there!"

"Miner's ghost, it's the miner's ghost, he's real, he's really real!" Jilly ran in place, not able to contain her nervous excitement. "Let's get out of here!"

We were freaked out as we scrambled away from the swing set and ran around Central. We paused before passing in front of the high school, peaking around the corner to see if the miner's ghost had gone back into hiding. "Wait a minute," I came to a stop and grabbed Jilly's arm. I studied the window on the front door. "I think we should look inside," I whispered.

"Are you nuts? There is no way I am going near that school. I can't believe you want to!" She looked at me as though I had two heads. We stood on the boulevard and studied the front door. I added another piece of gum to the existing wad, bringing a burst of bubblegum flavor inside my mouth which made it water.

"Come on! Let's just look in the front door. Do you really think it's a ghost?" I joked nervously and blew a huge bubble. My curiosity was overriding my fear and I needed to take advantage of my unexpected bravery. I'm not sure why I suddenly had the guts to look inside the old high school that day, or what I thought I'd find, but for some reason I had courage, and something compelled me to walk up those steps.

66

I grabbed Jilly's hand as we crouched down and walked up toward the immense front doors. We hunkered below the window, counted to three and slowly raised our heads high enough to peek inside. My eyes scanned the long hallway that led to the classrooms on the backside of the building. It was difficult to see, since the other windows were boarded up and this door provided the only light source in the hallway. I examined the wooden staircase leading down to the lower floor, looking for any signs of a ghostly miner.

My eyes were glued to the bottom of the steps when a shadow quickly flit past. Jilly gasped. We turned and looked at each other, our eyes bugging out of our heads. Slowly we looked back at the staircase, but my eyes started to water because I was trying to hold them still without blinking, for fear of missing a glimpse. We stood like statues for what seemed like an eternity. All that nervous waiting made me have to go to the bathroom.

"Let's go," I whispered.

We stayed crouched down and decided to leave by crawling across the lawn toward the street, in case something or someone was watching out the front window through the cracks in the boards. We stood up and darted from tree to tree like we saw cowboys do in the movies. "Run!" I urged, and we started running toward our houses.

"Do you think that was the ghost of the dead miner?" Jilly panted as we ran.

"I don't know, I thought ghosts were white like a cloud. That looked darker, like a shadow," I gulped a breath of air. I got the chills just thinking about it. I would surely need to leave the light on in my room for a few

Sounds of Home

more days.

CHAPTER 9

Roo had been rehearsing her flower girl routine ever since our oldest sister, Karoline, told her she would have an important job in her August wedding. Her tattered blankie served as a veil for her head and her Halloween princess costume with the pink plastic, too small, high heel shoes, made up the rest of her ensemble.

She would collect small items like grass, leaves, or pebbles, and put them in her Easter basket and proceed to fling them out as she sang *Here Comes the Bride*. Unfortunately, the only version of that song that Roo knew was the one that I had taught her, so Roo would sashay down the sidewalk in front of our house, singing at the top of her lungs:

> *"Here comes the bride, big fat and wide!*
>
> *Where is the gro-ooom? He's in the bathroom!"*

The neighbors would smile and say things like, "How darling," until they heard what she was saying.

Mrs. Peters heard her practicing one day and of course she didn't think it was darling at all. "Little girl! Little girl!" she yelled across the street, waving her broom. We had lived across the street from her for two years and she still didn't know our names. "Stop that! Where is your mother?" She shook her head and resumed sweeping her walk, mumbling something about kids not having any respect these days.

We weren't sure if the wedding would take place at all, though, because Karoline and her fiancé' had a big argument while they were on a date, a few weeks back. When he pulled his orange Corvette into our driveway, Karoline got out of the car and slammed the door. She stomped toward the house, but suddenly stopped mid stride and tugged on her diamond engagement ring. After a few grunts, she yanked it off her finger, and threw it at him through the car window. She screamed, "The wedding is off! I never want to see you again!"

"Hey, that ring's expensive!" he shrieked, his voice reaching an octave higher. He shook his head knowing it would do no good to argue. He sped off and Karoline ran crying up to her room and slammed the door. The whole scene, an Emmy winner for *All My Children*.

When Roo heard what had happened, she was devastated that her shining moment of being a flower girl might not happen. But Roo was quite the actress herself; she was good, real good. She was destined for the big screen, and as she stood outside Karoline's doorway on a mission to change her mind about getting married, she inhaled deeply and breathed out a long slow breath and went in for the kill.

Karoline was sitting on the edge of her bed. Roo

grasped Karoline's face into her chubby little hands and pulled her close. I'm sure Karoline could smell the Fruity Pebbles from this morning's breakfast on Roo's breath. "Karoline, you *have* to get married! I want to be a flower girl," she whimpered. She blinked her eyes and big tears rolled down her face, still holding Karoline's cheeks and looking directly into her eyes. She sniffed dramatically.

As I watched her crocodile tears drip onto Karoline's legs, I thought even if she didn't love the guy, Karoline should have gotten married anyway, so this pitiful little flower girl could have her shining moment in the sun.

"I don't think..." Karoline started to shake her head in protest, but Roo wouldn't let her finish the sentence. Roo's expression turned from sadness to fury in a split second. Catching Karoline off guard, Roo suddenly flung herself down on the floor and proceeded to wail, pounding her arms and legs on the shag carpet, which was something she would have done when she was two or three, not six. It was interesting though; the crocodile tears had gone dry. I rolled my eyes at Karoline and left the room. Karoline began to paint her nails, totally ignoring the bad acting scene taking place on her bedroom floor.

Finally, when Roo decided her audience just wasn't interested, she stood up and stomped out of Karoline's room as though she were crushing cans, nail polish bottles on the dresser clinking as she thundered past. At the door, she turned toward Karoline, a look of indignation on her face, and repeated a line from a movie she had seen, that I know she was saving for a moment just like this. "Frankly, my dear, I don't give a damn!" and slammed the door, causing the hallway mirror to bounce against the wall. I winced preparing for the sound of shattering glass.

"Roo!" my mom called instantaneously from the kitchen.

Little Scarlet O'Hara squeaked, "Yes Mommy," and oh so quietly, tiptoed down the stairs, trying not to ruffle any more of my mom's feathers.

Whether Roo had anything to do with it or not, the happy couple was back together by the next afternoon. We tore that Corvette apart looking for Karoline's diamond ring and it was nowhere to be found. We looked all over the driveway, in the bushes, the grass, but the ring was never to be seen again.

I pictured the future owner of the Corvette freaking out after discovering a diamond ring under his car mat. Of course, Karoline was bestowed a new ring, bigger and better than the one before, and both she and Roo were content with the way things worked out.

CHAPTER 10

My mom was across the street speaking to Mrs. Peters when I woke up the next morning. Mrs. Peters sat on her porch swing dabbing her eyes with a handkerchief.

I really wanted to go over and listen to their conversation, but I didn't want to miss *The Archie's,* on Saturday morning cartoons, and of course, *American Bandstand* would be aired directly afterward. I loved Saturday morning cartoons, especially, *The Archie's.* Jilly and I played their record over and over in my basement and became *The Archie's,* using tennis rackets as guitars. Jilly and I would argue over who got to be Veronica, but Jilly's long dark hair was a closer match, so she was usually Veronica. Betty would have to be blonde with a pixie cut.

A commercial came on and I went back to the window. Mom was heading across the street to our house. Her head down, she rubbed the back of her neck as she came inside.

"Is everything okay with Mrs. Peters?" I asked. My dad had been sitting in the living room reading the newspaper and looked up to listen.

Mom let out a deep sigh and folded her arms.

"Mrs. Peters received a telegram from the Army. Jesse is officially MIA. That poor woman has not heard from her grandson for months," she sighed. "I wish there was something we could do."

I knew what MIA meant, *Missing in Action*. It was almost worse than being killed in action because some soldiers would be lost forever, and their families would live a lifetime and never find out what had happened to their sons.

My dad stood up and jingled the change in his pocket, a habit he had when he was nervous or in rare moments when he was angry. There were no words to be said. He had been a fighting Seabee during WWII and knew very well about the traumas of war. Dad had never spoken about the time he served in the Pacific, and his memories were locked deep inside. We had no idea what he had been through and I wondered if news about Jesse would unleash any long-lost sentiments.

I looked out our front window to see if Mrs. Peters was sitting on her radiator by her front window, but it was empty.

I went to the backyard and sat on the stoop. Skip came and sat next to me and nudged my hand for a pet. As I sat there thinking about Jesse and his grandmother, my dog sensed I needed a friend and sat down by my side. Losing a first a son, then her husband, and now a grandson, would be enough for anyone to go madly insane.

I thought back to the first time I had met Jesse. The November after we moved into our house on Warren Street, our town was hit by a raging snowstorm. I went outside to shovel our front walk for the second time that night. Skip came to keep me company.

I was just about finished shoveling the walk when Skip spotted something and darted off. I yelled for him to come back, but of course he didn't listen. Snow began to fall, and he had run clear up the block. I could see his tracks in the snow. "Skip! Skip! Go to the lake? C'mon boy!" I yelled, but my voice was muffled by the wind. I held my mittened hands up to shield the snow from my eyes, but Skip was nowhere to be seen.

I followed his tracks about three blocks before I had to stop and dig snow out of my boot. I popped a frozen piece of bubblegum into my mouth, which was more like a jawbreaker than gum at that point. The biting wind whipped frozen snow crystals that felt like shards of glass hitting my frozen cheeks and chin. I wound my waist length stocking cap wound around my neck and chin for protection.

I finally heard a faint whimper. "Skip! I yelled and ran toward the sound. "C'mon fella, c'mon boy," I coaxed.

He limped toward me, but finally sat down, not able to go another step. "Oh, buddy, you're hurt." The pads of his feet were caked with snow. I hoisted him into my arms but could only carry him a few steps before I had to sit down and readjust his weight. This was going to be difficult to pack him home. My fingers were so numb from the biting cold and Skip wasn't a petite dog.

I kneeled on the sidewalk readying myself to stand. The blowing snow was like shrapnel in my eyes and blurred my vision. I squinted, trying to look through the sea of white, and realized someone was approaching.

"Who is that, Skip?" I whispered in his ear and hugged him close. I decided I'd better get up and try carrying him again, but he was just too heavy for me to manage.

"Hey, are you okay?" a muffled voice called through the din. He must have seen my blank expression. "It's okay, I'm Jesse Peters... from across the street..." he continued, "the Peters' grandson."

I looked at him with relief. He held his arms out to grab Skip and I gladly handed my shaking dog over to him. "Yes, thank you, I didn't know if I was going to make it all the way home."

"We'd better get you two home, right fella?" he looked at Skip. Skip licked his face and Jesse laughed. Skip relaxed and laid his head on Jesse's shoulder as we continued walking.

"My mom said you are leaving for boot camp after Christmas?" I yelled through the wind.

"Yep, I have to be on the bus in Butte by the 26th," he yelled back.

We walked in an uncomfortable silence for the next block. To me, being drafted to Vietnam meant I would probably never see him again. I wasn't quite sure what to say, but then opened my mouth, "Are you scared to go to Vietnam?" I was not yelling anymore.

I didn't think he had heard me, because he kept walking, but then he stopped and looked at me. "Betts, I suppose I would be lying if I told you I wasn't scared. I'm sure everybody who has gone to Vietnam, has a deep-down fear that they may not return."

"Why do you have to go? I heard there are lots of guys heading to Canada to get out of going to Vietnam. Some people are burning their draft cards," I covered my mouth with my stocking cap tail, catching the moisture from my nose.

"First of all, it's my turn, and secondly, if not me, then who will else will help save the world?" he smiled. Although he was trying to make light of the question, we both knew the seriousness of the situation, and right then, I thought he was the bravest person I had ever met.

In the month that followed, Jesse could be found pulling neighborhood kids on sleds down the street, making complex snow forts with us, and shoveling snow for some of the older people on the block. The most memorable day was the mega-snowball fight that all started with Jesse throwing a single snowball at Jilly and me that evolved to epic proportions. More and more kids joined in, along with a few parents that had no choice, but to join, when they got caught in the crossfire exiting their vehicles after work. Snowballs were flying across Warren Street from house to house as cars sped by like ducks in a carnival shooting game. That day will be forever etched in my memory.

My thoughts of that first winter with Jesse were interrupted by a magpie squawking on the fence. "Where are you, Jesse?" I said out loud. My mind pictured him wandering lost in a jungle, but the reality was, he probably was not wandering. I blinked the water free from my eyes and laid my chin on my arms. Skip cocked his head to one side and proceeded to lick my cheek. I put my arm around his neck and wiped my face in his fur. "How could that be?" I whispered. "How could someone from my neighborhood be missing? That only happened on TV, to strangers who lived far, far away."

Skip suddenly raised his head and darted to the fence when we heard Mr. Magoo rev his engine across the alley. Mr. Magoo was the name of a cartoon character that Jilly and I had given to our neighbor, Randy Block. Mr. Block was in his late eighties and had poor eyesight. He was as blind as a bat, and older than my house, but he still drove his 1955 green Studebaker. He would get into all kinds of trouble because of his bad vision, and often he was completely oblivious to the outcome. He could barely see over the dashboard of his car, so when he drove down our alley, it looked like a hat was driving his car.

On this day, as he backed out into the alley, he hit the neighbor's metal garbage can. Of course, he had no clue that the metal can was rolling and clanking down the alley, spewing its contents all over the dusty gravel. Mr. Magoo just rolled on down the alley in his little green car. As he turned onto the street, I heard a horn honk and the screeching of tires. "Look out Helena, Magoo is on the loose," I said to myself.

CHAPTER 11

The following Monday was a scorcher, a record setting 99 degrees. During baton lessons at Memorial Park, we had to stop and run through the sprinklers to cool down. Alvin happened to be adjusting the sprinkler and aimed it at us causing us to shriek when the freezing water hit our baking skin. He laughed and stood up, running a hand through his dark, Beatles-style haircut. "What's Winnie up to today?" he yelled over the chatter of the sprinkler.

"Babysitting, as usual!" I yelled back.

"Tell her I said, hello!" he smiled and walked off to adjust the next sprinkler.

Jilly and I looked at each other and giggled. I had to respect him for still being interested in a girl who wore Cool Whip on her face and macaroni necklaces for jewelry.

The bike ride home from the park was uphill all the way. Our stingray bikes had no gears, so by the time we had pedaled the five blocks to our houses in the scorching sun, our hair plastered the sides of our cherry red cheeks. We stopped at my house to guzzle a drink of water from the hose, and Jilly and I decided the Memorial Park Pool would be a good idea after lunch.

As I walked in the front door, Audrey March was crying again in front of the nurse's station of *General Hospital*. Roo was intently working her beautician skills on Winnie. Winnie's long thick hair had about twenty little ponytails randomly placed around her head, as though they were seedlings sprouting from the soil. They both looked up when I walked in the door.

"Alvin said to say hello to you!" I said in a sing song voice.

Winnie looked up with a smirk on her face and shook her head. I could tell she was secretly happy about my comment, because of the crooked smile on her face. Then, after I had gone into the kitchen to make my lunch, she yelled from the living room, "What else did he say?"

Roo immediately chimed in, "Ooh, two little lovebirds sitting in a tree, k-i-s-s-i-n-g, first comes love, then comes marriage, then mmphff…"

Winnie covered Roo's mouth with her hand, "That's not nice to tease people, Roo." But then after a minute went by, "Well… did he?" she half laughed and looked toward the kitchen door.

"Nope," I shook my head.

I smiled and went to make a bologna sandwich with potato chips stuck in between. "Betts," Winnie called from the living room, don't forget you need to vacuum and dust before mom gets home."

"Ugh, I'll do it when I get home from swimming," I grumbled. We were in charge of cleaning the house while my parents were at work. We basically needed to clean up after ourselves, things like vacuuming, dusting, and doing the dishes. It wasn't a lot, but we avoided it as long as we possibly could… every single day.

Our mom was a pediatric nurse at Shodair Children's Hospital, which was a one-minute walk home. We could see the front door of the hospital from our house, which worked to our benefit. The minute we saw the white nurse's cap and uniform heading across the park, it would be at that moment we would start hustling to clean up. Sometimes desperate times would call for desperate measures, and we wouldn't have enough time to vacuum or dust, so we would use the carpet rake to fluff up the shag carpeting in our living and dining rooms, and then spray Pledge in the air, like it was air freshener.

My mom was well-aware of our cleaning methods but would always have high hopes of us getting it done the next day, because of Winnie's Catholic guilt complex. Sooner or later Winnie would feel bad that we had let mom down and make us do the real cleaning.

That afternoon, Memorial Park Pool was packed with kids who were trying to escape the heat of the hot Montana summer. The water wasn't as shockingly cold as the lake near my family's summer cabin, but its clear blue water was enticing as the smell of the chlorine filled the air.

I loved diving down to touch the bottom of the pool or handstand contests with Jilly, because you could clearly see where you were going, unlike the green algae colored water at the lake. The downside of swimming in the city pool, was having red burning eyes afterward from the germ-killing amounts of chlorine that was added. Kids with red eyes in 1970, had either been swimming at the city pool or were stoned.

Jilly and I typically wore our swimsuits under our clothes, so we wouldn't have to undress in the women's locker room, because the few stalls that were provided usually had waiting lines. We didn't like taking the required showers either, because God knows what you would see in there that could never be erased from your memory. I didn't mind seeing the young babies in their birthday suits, but inevitably there would be an old grandma shuffling in to take a shower and my eyes weren't quite ready to see that.

The only thing we brought were our towels and swim caps. The required swim cap was a major pain, because it was made from rubber and pulled my hair when I tried to put it on. Worse yet, nobody looked good in a swim cap.

After we put our clothes in the baskets and checked them in with the attendant, we found a place for our towels and headed for the high dive. The best part about Memorial Park Pool was the high dive diving board. We liked to dare each other to jump off without holding our noses. It seemed so high up when we stood on the edge of the board and looked down at the people in the water below. Making such a leap of faith was a rite of passage for any kid that hung around the pool in the summer.

We went to the end of the long line to wait for our turn behind some younger boys. One young boy ahead of me, who looked to be about five years old, was telling his friends an old legend that never seemed to die.

The legend involved a group of high school kids who climbed the chain link fence surrounding the pool one night. They were drinking Mad Dog 20/20, or maybe it was Boone's Farm. One boy staggered over to the high dive while his friends were soaking and drinking at the shallow end of the pool. As he staggered to the edge of the high dive, he slipped and hit his head on the diving board and knocked himself out. He sank like a stone to the bottom of the pool.

Meanwhile, the other kids had no idea where he had gone. Come to find out, the next morning when the lifeguards opened the pool, they found his body floating under the high dive. Dead as a door nail. Supposedly, he haunts the pool each night when the sun goes down.

That story always gave me the creeps and I was never quite sure how much of it was truth, or if any of it was truth. Jilly and I thought the pool authorities created the legend to keep kids from climbing the fence when the pool was closed.

The little five-year-old telling the story was missing his front teeth, and had difficulty saying his s's and r's, so his version of the story went more like:

"Hey guyths, did you know thew was a guy, who fewl off the diving boawd and dwounded? "Nobody can thwim hew at night becauth he turnded into a ghotht and will haunt you fowevew."

The other little wide-eyed five-year-olds listening to his interpretation of the story, with mouths agape, stared at the storyteller with wonder and awe. But, then one of them frowned and said, "No way!"

"Honeth guyths, ith the twuth, I thwear!" he put

his hand up as though he were reciting an oath in front of a courtroom judge, eyes wide with seriousness.

"I ain't jumping into that water! I'm getting out of here!" a little redhead yelled, and all of them started pushing and shoving each other as they tried to skedaddle away from the high dive, causing a ruckus. The lifeguards blew their whistles and yelled at them to stop running, which only happened when they reached the safety of their sunbathing mothers at the shallow end.

I was trying not to think of the dead guy, but I kept wondering if it was true, and if so, had this water had been changed since then? I mean, it supposedly happened in the 60's, this had to be fresh water, right?

Since the little boys chickened out, it was my turn on the high dive. I swallowed and started climbing the tall ladder and, as usual, began reciting the *Hail Mary*. It was needed. Frankly, I was scared and wanted to run to the little boys' mothers, too. As I got to the top, I paused and tried to calm myself. I must have been up there for a while because Jilly got impatient and yelled, "Jump, Betts!"

That caught the attention of other people in the pool, even through the squeals and shouts of the swimmers. Suddenly, everyone was staring at me, and I froze with embarrassment. I had stood on that board so many times before, scared out of my wits, but I had still jumped. Now, everyone in the pool seemed to be watching me as I stewed about jumping into the blue water.

Soon, the little kids from the shallow end who went crying to their mommies, chimed in, "JUMP! JUMP! JUMP!" It was hard to concentrate while Alvin and the Chipmunks chirped like they had just found a golden acorn.

I looked out toward the park and saw Alvin outside the chain link fence, watering the new trees near the diving area. His interest apparently had been peaked from the commotion inside the pool. His eyes locked with mine. He saw my panic. I could see his head nod through the din, and then he made a diving motion with his hands.

"I can do this," I said to myself, "one, two... and by the time I hit three I had gotten hold of my senses, stepped off the board and made a grand splash in the pool. I sank to the bottom, pushed off the smooth cement, and burst like a rocket toward the air at the top. As I reached the surface, I exhaled, thankful that I had once again survived a jump from the high dive and swam quickly to the concrete edge.

I looked around and saw that people had gone about swimming. The chipmunks had lost interest and were happily screaming and splashing away, thank the lord.

Jilly and I got out of the pool to lay on the hot concrete surrounding the pool. "Well, that was embarrassing," I muttered. Jilly just laughed and closed her eyes. The warmth of the concrete felt good as we laid there soaking up the sun.

I watched a little wren land on the chain link fence and proceed to swoop down to the moist grass near a sprinkler. It was being showered with sparkling drops of water at the edge of the sprinkler's range and it fluttered and shivered as each cold drop touched its tiny feathery frame. Such a delicate little thing, that a single drop of water could make such a difference.

Suddenly, it flitted away as a Frisbee flew

overhead. It came from a teenage boy who had thrown the Frisbee way over his friend's head. I watched it land near the feet of a man sitting in the shade of a sagging pine tree. The man hadn't been paying attention to the kids and flinched when the Frisbee hit near his foot. He lowered his head below the branches to see who owned the Frisbee. Instead of grabbing it, he just sat there staring at the boy who ran all the way over under the tree to pick it up. They didn't acknowledge each other; the boy just ran off.

He sat back against the tree and laid his head against the trunk. I propped my hands under my chin to get a better look at him. He looked like he may have come from the homeless shelter downtown. His baggy green pants needed washing, along with the rest of his clothing, and his five o'clock shadow was a few days old. Unlike others that wandered our neighborhood who were down on their luck, his hair was buzzed, as my dad would call it, high and tight. I raised my head to get a better look between two of the branches that partially hid him. It finally dawned on me; he was the guy from the church.

"Jilly," I whispered. No answer. "Jilly," I said a little louder and tapped her shoulder, as her left eye squinted opened. She had obviously been in a deep sleep from the drool that was seeping down her chin.

"What?" she croaked.

"That's the guy from the church," I was hiding my pointing finger with my other hand.

"What guy?" She lifted herself up on to one elbow.

"The guy that was at the church when we were playing Kick the Can the other night. He saved me from

86

being pulverized by Harvey Dill." We laid there and watched him. His eyes seemed to be staring off into space like he was in deep thought. People passing by didn't notice him, maybe because the branches of the tree were almost touching the ground making a perfect shaded umbrella for him. He didn't seem to notice the activity of the people in the park or in the noisy swimming pool. His eyes closed again, and he pulled his knees up to his chest, crossing his arms on top, letting his chin on top of his arms. After a while, he let out a long slow breath and started to get up.

"What's his story," I wondered aloud, "he looks so dang familiar." Helena was a small town, and people knew their neighbors, but I couldn't quite place him. "He still looks sad." I tapped Jilly's arm, "Hey, do you want to follow him?"

As we grabbed our towels and hustled toward the locker room. The lifeguard blew her whistle because we were breaking the running rule, but we just kept speed walking by her. "Ladies! Ladies! You girls stop running!" she yelled, but we were in the locker room by the time she started down from her tower. Deciding we were too fast and already in the locker room, she just shook her head and climbed back into the lifeguard's chair.

We handed the locker room attendant the safety pins with our basket number etched on them and grabbed our clothes. We quickly threw our t-shirts and shorts on over our suits and ripped the caps off our heads and ran barefoot out of the pool building, holding our moccasins and towels.

"Do you see him?" Jilly asked as we ran around the corner of the building into the park. Our eyes scanned the direction we had last seen him.

"There he is, across the park by the warming house. C'mon," I motioned, and we ran toward the warming house. We stopped and hid by the corner of the building, so he wouldn't see us. We watched him cross Euclid Avenue and go up an alley behind the houses on Warren Street. We were still in our bare feet as we headed up the alley, darting behind garages and garbage cans to hide from his sight.

Our feet were as tough as leather. It wasn't unusual for us to walk downtown or to Memorial Park in our bare feet, over hot concrete sidewalks and asphalt streets, so running down the rocky alley was not a problem, either. If we had to wear shoes, moccasins were the next best thing to bare feet.

He kept walking up the alley, nearing our houses, his head down, as though he didn't want to make eye contact with anyone walking the opposite way. I heard Skip's deep growl, as he peered through the cracks in the fence at the stranger walking past our yard.

We ditched our towels and shoes in my backyard. Skip, of course, wanted to come with us, and he began barking frantically and jumping on the fence, more than his usual ruckus. "Quiet Skip," I whispered, and we crouched out of sight. "Stay! Stay in the yard!"

As we started up the alley, I could hear Skip's paws, clawing their way up the six-foot fence. That dog was like Spider Man, he could scale tall objects even when there was nothing to grasp onto.

"Argh! I'm going to have to go put him inside," I muttered. "Keep following him," I whispered, "I'll catch up." Jilly nodded silently as she stood behind the Fay's garage.

I darted back into my yard and grabbed Skip by the collar. Of course, he knew he was going inside the house, the very last place he wanted to be, so he planted all four of his feet in the grass. He would not budge, even though I was tugging him by the collar. He even started yelping, to make me think I was hurting him. But then he did the very move that I hated, he rolled on his back and played dead, limp body literally impossible to move. His tongue dangled out of the side of his mouth and wild eyes completed the dead dog aura.

"Dang it," I muttered. I hated to do it, but "Skip, go to the lake? Go to the lake?" I enthusiastically slapped my legs and started running up the stairs to the back door. He heard my excitement, legs flailing in the air trying to make their way to the ground beneath him. After a few seconds of air running, his legs found their way to solid ground, and he bounded after me into the house.

I yelled toward the living room as I was closing the door to Skip's sad face, "Don't let Skip out, he's trying to jump the fence," and slammed the door and ran toward the alley. I could hear Winnie start to yell, "You need to vac..." before the door slammed shut.

I peeked around the corner to see Jilly zigzagging across the alley on the next block. I ran to catch up, prepared to quickly dart behind something if the guy turned around. Frankly, I was amazed he was still calmly walking up the alley after Skip's freak out barking episode.

But, as I watched Jilly sneaking from one side of the alley to the other on her tiptoes, it reminded me of

Sylvester the Cat when he was sneaking up on Tweety Bird. During the TV cartoon, at some point, Tweety Bird would get suspicious and say, "I tot I taw a puddy tat! Did I? Did I tee a puddy tat?"

I started to laugh picturing the stranger imitating Tweety Bird, "I tot I taw a wittle girl! Did I?"

Trying to run and laugh at the same time, just made me laugh harder and louder. I was holding my hand over my mouth trying to will myself to shut up, but it only caused bubblegum slobber to soak my palms. My eyes were blurry with tears as I laughed, watching Jilly darting to and fro. I swear I could hear the plunking of piano keys, with each step she took, like they do in the cartoons.

Finally, she turned around because she could hear my lame attempts to suppress my laughter. She motioned for me to come quickly, while holding her other index finger to her mouth to shush me. I lifted the bottom of my shirt to wipe my nose and eyes and made a mental note that this shirt had probably lived enough life between washings, and I would have to throw it down the chute to the laundry room tonight when I changed for bed.

Jilly had a quizzical look on her face. "What the...?" she mouthed the words.

"Don't ask," I said. The look on her face was most likely wondering if I had gone mad. "Which way did he go?" and I made another unsuccessful attempt to stifle another fit of laughter.

"I think he's heading toward Central," Jilly surmised, and we made a dash across the parking lot and climbed the grassy hill of the Cathedral. We hid behind the towering corner of the front doors and watched him walk to the back of the old abandoned high school. Making a run for it across the street, we climbed the stone wall that surrounded the old high school and ran toward the back. We flattened ourselves against the stone wall and slid with our backs along the bumpy stones. Jilly and I made eye contact and I nodded for her to peek around the corner. I was breathless and could feel my heart beating as she inched around the corner.

Jilly hadn't looked for more than two seconds and quickly jumped back. She mouthed the words, "I think he's inside the building," in an exaggerated way.

I apparently had been holding my breath because I suddenly let all the air out of my mouth, which made a giant "Phhhffft," even though I had both of my hands over my mouth, trying to stifle the exhaling air from my lungs. It was no use, and Jilly knew exactly what was coming next, my uncontrolled nervous laughter. She put her hand over my mouth as I crouched down desperately trying to suppress my laughter; tears rolling down my cheeks.

I have been known to laugh at the most inopportune times... church, school, family dinner at Jilly's house. Once, Jilly's mom invited both Winnie and me to have dinner with their family. Remember, they are a family with four well-mannered girls. My family of six kids, we were okay-mannered, but a little livelier at the dinner table. Having six kids in the family, with two of them growing boys, made for some fast eating to make sure second helpings were still available.

When we sat down at Jilly's antique dinner table, I noticed a bowl of the biggest kernels of corn I had ever seen in my life. My eyes grew wide, and I looked at

Winnie, thinking, "Jackpot on the corn!" For some reason she was staring straight at me and knew exactly what I was thinking that I couldn't wait to get a mouthful of that juicy corn! She shook her head in the smallest way, so that only I would see. I made a questioning frown at her as I placed my napkin on my lap, wondering what she was trying to tell me.

Mr. Gardner started dishing up his plate and passed the bowls of food around the table. I took an extra big helping of the giant corn, because I loved corn, and was anxious to try its juicy goodness. No one spoke as we started eating, which magnified the gentle clanking of forks as they scooped food off plates. The silence made me slightly nervous.

As I scooped the first mouthful of corn onto my fork, Winnie bit her bottom lip and raised her eyebrows, not taking her eyes off me. Her own forkful of potatoes suspended midway between her plate and her mouth, waiting for me to take a bite. I wondered why she was acting so weird but didn't care and shoved the huge corns into my mouth and started chewing, waiting for the corny goodness to fill my mouth.

Something wasn't right. I stopped chewing, thinking this did not taste like my mom's delicious, canned corn. As a matter of fact, I was getting a slight gag reflex, and stopped chewing. As the soggy contents sat in my mouth, I was praying I wouldn't hurl the corny mush across the table.

My eyes locked with Winnie's as a slow smile spread across her face. She was biting her lip trying not to smile, looking up toward the ceiling, hoping to avoid my lack of corn chewing. I could see her shoulders start to shake in a silent laugh, and her eyes begin to water. She tried her hardest to not look at me and to eat her own forkful of mashed potatoes. She put her napkin to her mouth trying to suppress her ridiculous smile and stifle her laugh. Of course, the silence made it worse. I too, began to lose it. As I attempted to mush the corn substance in my mouth enough to swallow, tears were welling up in my eyes.

Of course, the whole family was on to me right away, and burst out laughing. Jilly asked if I knew I was eating hominy, not regular corn. I made an exaggerated gulp, and finally swallowed the mouthful of hominy, followed by a huge swallow of water. "No, I have never heard of hominy. I thought this giant corn may have come from the Jolly Green Giant's garden." Everyone laughed, including Mr. and Mrs. Gardner.

Now, as I was standing near the old high school, I needed to get myself under control, because if the guy inside heard me burst into a laughing fit, who knew what would happen? I didn't think he would be as understanding as Jilly's family. I quickly regained control as we started belly crawling toward the window.

There was a loose board leaning against the window, so we were able to see through the side cracks. Jilly and I both had our faces right next to the board as we were peering in, trying to get our eyes to adjust to the darkness. Suddenly, I lost my balance and fell into the deep window well.

"Jilly!" I screamed in a panic. I was scrambling trying to get to my feet, but there was gravel at the bottom of the well and my frenzied movement to regain my stance, made me slip even more. The stone window well surpassed the height of my head, so climbing the gray stones would require Jilly's assistance.

Jilly reached into the window well to grab my hand, and suddenly, we heard a raspy voice, "Why are you following me?"

I jumped, and all the blood drained from my head. I felt dizzy and thought I was going to faint, wondering if I was going to make it out alive.

Jilly chimed in, "Stay away, or I'm going to the cops right now! I mean it!"

"Jilly, don't leave me," I whispered, "I'm scared."

CHAPTER 12

"Why are you following me," he repeated. He was still on the other side of the broken window from me, obviously not even attempting to come closer.

Jilly and I locked eyes trying to read each other's thoughts, eyebrows raised. Jilly was trying to pull me out of the window well, but our hasty attempt caused me to fall again. We both turned back to look at him. He grimaced as though either he was in pain, or he felt the pain of my fall.

I decided he didn't look that threatening, and I could probably take him with a kick to his privates. "Are you hurt or something?" I asked, standing up and brushing the dirt off my cut-offs, still on guard, ready to scramble out of the window well. He didn't answer, but just stared at me. I squinted my eyes, and got up the nerve to ask, "Were you in the church the other day?" He glanced up at me to study my face. It was him.

He looked rough, really rough, and as I studied his tired eyes, it finally dawned on me… "Jesse?" We both stood staring at each other, until he turned away with both hands-on top of his head. He let out a huge breath of air. Nobody spoke until I finally blurted out, "I didn't realize it was you without your long hair and beard! You... you look so, so... different," my voice trailed off.

"Your grandma has been really worried about you. Everybody has been wor...," I suddenly stopped, realizing this wasn't right. I turned to try and climb the rocky wall. Jilly reached down and successfully pulled me out of the window well. We sat on our heels looking over its ledge, wondering why was he hiding out at the old school instead of going home?

He let out an exhausted sigh. "It's a long story..."

"Jesse? Your grandma..." I was confused.

"Listen," he began, "I know my grandmother is concerned about me," he took a deep breath, "but, please, for now, don't tell her you saw me. It would upset her. Things aren't what they seem."

"Are you in some kind of trouble?" I asked.

His lack of answer left me wondering. We knew that AWOL meant Absent Without Leave, and soldiers who left without permission could be sent to prison for many years. We were quiet trying to absorb this new information to make sense of it.

I opened my mouth, wanting to ask him what happened, but it wouldn't say the words. My mom once told me that soldiers returning home from war needed to make peace in their own time. It would be rude to ask a veteran for all the details of their deployment, like how many men they killed, especially if you yourself had never witnessed the horrors of war.

Jesse eventually climbed out of the window well, and we all sat there in the shade of the old high school, looking over downtown Helena and farther beyond to the whitewashed H on Mt. Helena. He seemed to settle back, grateful for our company and our silence.

I squinted upward into the azure blue back drop at an osprey whistling overhead. Perched on a dead branch at the top of a huge pine tree, it watched the cars on the street as though they were trout swimming downstream. It must have realized dinner was not to be, and lit off the branch, wings gracefully flapping to gain altitude, soaring upward into the blue. We were all entranced as it aligned higher than the Cathedral spires, stretching its wings to spiral downward in effortless lazy circles along the breezes above the Battlefield, the nickname school children had given our playground decades prior. A sudden gust reversed the osprey's course and sent it away toward Mount Helena.

Jesse broke the silence, "The larks, still bravely singing, fly scarce heard amid the guns below..." he whispered as his eyes followed the osprey until it was a speck in the atmosphere.

"We are the Dead. Short days ago." I quietly continued the recitation, watching the osprey completely disappear. *Flanders Fields* was a poem we had memorized and recited in Mrs. Holt's class, "We lived, felt dawn, saw sunset glow, loved and were loved..."

Jesse's raspy voice was barely audible as he joined me, "and now we lie in Flanders Fields."

I swallowed hard, thinking that I finally understood what the poem was trying to say. The larks could still be slightly heard above the gunfire on the battlefield below, signaling hope, but not for the soldiers, who, just days before the battle, had a life full of love and enjoyed the beauty of the world, but were now buried beneath the blowing poppies.

Jesse eyes were glistening, I swallowed the lump in my throat. I had never seen a grown man cry, not my brothers or my dad, and I wasn't quite sure what to do. I pulled my knees up to my chest, trying to blink away the pools of water forming in my own eyes.

"The air just sucked my breath away when we stepped off that plane, it was so hot and humid," Jesse shook his head, his eyes far away. "It seemed too thick, and the air had a hard time finding its way into my lungs, nothing like Montana. It was quite a shock. I never did get use to that."

"There was talk that we were going to abandon the base, but we continued to fight, until the official orders to evacuate came over the radio." He paused and looked off in the distance and wiped his nose with the back of his hand. "We waited too long..."

I had the feeling he was about to tell us something awful, but we suddenly heard voices. Jesse was jolted back to the present and looked up, quickly scanning the surrounding area. He slipped through the window in one swift motion and Jilly and I secured the board in front of it. We ran off around the far side of the building toward the swings. I felt the rapid pulse of my heart from the quick action to hide Jesse and rubbed my hands together to keep them from shaking.

CHAPTER 13

"Wow," was all Jilly could say as she looked at me. We saw the redness in each other's eyes. The ache I was feeling reminded me of the pain I felt when my mom told me Grandma had died. It was deep inside and just plain took my breath away. I wiped my nose with the back of my hand and bent my head to wipe my eyes on the shoulder of my shirt.

Right about then we watched Tommy Benson and Sean Wilson come around the corner of Central School. Tommy and Sean had been our friends for most of elementary school. They may have referred to us as being their girlfriends, but we referred to them as boys that were friends. Big difference, especially if you asked our parents. Although, my parents had no idea that boys were in our group of friends. I wasn't about to share this information with anyone in my family, the consequences would be disastrous.

Being the fifth of six kids was a precarious family position. I wasn't the cute little one, like Roo, who for some reason could charm my brothers' friends into letting her tag along when they drove the drag down Helena

Avenue. They would enter our house, and we both could be sitting in the living room, but somehow, Roo magically drew them into her cuteness.

" Hey Roo, want to be my date tonight?" one would say, as I became the invisible girl sitting right next to her.

"Yes!" she would smile, bouncing off the couch with her little Cindy Brady pigtails bobbing in unison. My shyness made it hard to compete with someone as adorable as that. I think my brothers knew it hurt my feelings, but their way of showing me affection was to punch me in the arm.

My older brothers and sisters also blessed me with a nickname that stuck like glue and will most likely end up on my tombstone. I happened to love watching the Andy Griffith TV show. Andy was the sheriff of the quaint southern town of Mayberry, so quaint in fact, he didn't even carry a gun. The characters on the show were quirky yet endearing. There was motherly Aunt Bee, Andy's obedient son, Opie, Barney Fife the bumbling deputy, Floyd the barber, Otis the drunk, Gomer Pyle, a simple-minded auto mechanic, and finally, my namesake, Goober, Gomer's simple-minded cousin who was also an auto mechanic.

Yep, Goober it was and Goober it forever stayed. Each time they called me Goober, I would go after them with arms swinging, in a chase around the house. The louder they laughed, the madder I would get, the madder I would get, the louder they laughed.

My mom gave me some great advice, "Betts, if you ignore them, they will quit." I'm still waiting for that advice to take effect. Thus, it would be later in my life that a first grandson would call for his Nana Goobie.

So, if any of my brothers or sisters had one inkling that I was hanging out with a boy, I would have to pack up and move far far away or be teased mercilessly forever and ever.

Sean and Tommy approached the swing set. "Why are you guys sitting here? This playground is hot as hell!" Tommy reckoned.

"Um, the pool was too crowded. Too many little rug rats," I replied quickly, hoping he wouldn't think it was weird we were sitting on a scorching hot playground in the midday sun.

"Uh, yeah, we should all go run through the sprinklers on the Cathedral lawn!" Jilly piped in. "C'mon," she hopped off the swing, hoping they would follow. My eyes darted toward the old high school. We didn't have a good view of the lower window from where we stood, but we needed them to follow us to the opposite side of Central, just in case. We probably could have trusted Sean and Tommy with Jesse's secret, but we promised Jesse we wouldn't tell anyone he was there.

"Wait, what time is it?" I suddenly panicked.

None of us wore watches, so we weren't quite sure. Right then, the Cathedral bells began chiming and we stopped to listen for the number of chimes. BONG... BONG... BONG... BO... In the middle of the fourth bong, I knew I was in trouble. I was supposed to vacuum the carpet and dust before my mom got off work at 4:00. Argh! She was probably walking across the park as we spoke. "I gotta go!" I started running down the sidewalk.

"See you guys later!"

Jilly yelled after me, "Call me after dinner, maybe we can sleep outside tonight!"

I raced down the four blocks to my house, looking toward the triangle park and beyond to Shodair Hospital, but saw no sign of my mom. "Phew," I panted, and went in the house.

CHAPTER 14

"Where have you been? You were supposed to..." Winnie started to say.

"Vacuum and dust, I know," still panting, and I ran to the closet to grab the vacuum, swallowing hard to catch my breath.

"Young lady, you are going to be in big, big trouble," Roo said in her best mom voice.

"Roo, quick, go look out the window to see if mom is coming," I ordered.

She just stood there with her hands on her hips and tapping her foot, still in her pretend mom mode. I softened my tone, "Please, Roo?" I smiled.

"Okay, I will, but young lady, you need to vacuum!" she scolded.

I glanced in the kitchen and Winnie was just filling the sink to start the dishes. She was darting back and forth grabbing dishes and towels trying to hurry. Apparently, the soap operas had kept her in their spell the whole afternoon, and she hadn't done her chores either. I didn't notice any remnants of a Roo Spa treatment, though, and Winnie actually looked normal today.

There was no time to vacuum, so I grabbed the carpet rake instead. Mom always wanted us to rake the shag carpeting after we vacuumed so it looked fluffy and new. Hopefully, with my raking treatment, the dog hair would be shuffled about, and Mom wouldn't notice Skip's summer shedding.

I was about halfway through the house when Roo screamed, "SHE'S COMING!! HURRY! HURRY! SHE'S COMING!" she kept repeating and jumping up and down and running from the front door to the kitchen.

Winnie and I turned to mock speed. Dishes were clanking and cupboard doors slamming, the *shush shush shush* of the carpet rake went faster and faster. I finally grabbed the Pledge and sprayed it in the air as though it was air freshener, and watched it settle on the dust of the console TV. We flew into the living room and sat down, trying to appear calm, the exact moment my mom opened the door.

"Hi Mom! What's for dinner?" I asked cheerily.

Winnie whacked my leg, "You know she hates that question the minute she walks in the door!" She turned her head and looked at Mom, "Hi Mom, how was your day?"

"Oh, it was busy," she unpinned her white nurse's hat from her head. "Every bed was full, we had four tonsillectomies today!"

"Oh, wow! You must be tired... um, what *is* for dinner?" Winnie asked right after. I gave her a sideways smirk.

It wasn't until I was a mom, that I realized my own mom was an amazing person. Her nursing job required eight hours of being on her feet consoling sick children, making beds, cleaning puke, comforting frightened parents, taking orders from impatient doctors, bed pan situations, and many other unseen duties. Then she would come home to six children and cook a dinner that usually included meat and potatoes, vegetables, bread, and some type of jello, day after day after day. On weekends, she would spend most of Saturday scrubbing floors, cleaning bedrooms, and doing the laundry. As a child, for the life of me, I never understood why she complained of being tired.

CHAPTER 15

All six kids were home for dinner that night, even Duke. My mom had fixed one of my favorites, round steak with mashed potatoes and gravy, green beans, and cherry jello with a pretzel crust and whip cream on top. I was eating fast because I wanted seconds of mashed potatoes and gravy.

Duke and Jack were both left-handed, and somehow my place at the table was right in between them. My right elbow kept colliding with Duke's left elbow, and every so often, my forkful of mashed potatoes would end up on my cheek or chin.

Jack looked up from his plate and said, "Charlie Andersen got an urgent call at work to go home," he took a big gulp of water. Charlie had been a classmate of Jack's through high school, and now they worked together delivering Coca Cola to businesses in town during the summer.

Everyone stopped eating and looked at him. Charlie's brother, Oly, had been in Vietnam for eight months. We all knew what Jack was going to say next. We had been watching news reports about the Vietnam War for over two years, and had seen the wounds, the protests, the flag draped coffins lined up in airport hangars, but one is never fully prepared to hear the ugly truths of war so close to their hometown.

"Oly is dead," Jack said.

We all stopped chewing mid-bite. My dad put down his fork and raised his elbows to the table clasping his hands together. After a short silence, he looked at Jack and said quietly, "I'm sorry to hear that, Jack," and he and my mom looked at each other. No one spoke for a long time. What were the appropriate words to use in times like these? It was painful, each time you heard the name of a hometown boy, that had succumbed to the harsh realities of a world that sucked innocent boys into its lair and spit them out like watermelon seeds. Taking a stand to defend what was right was coming at a high cost, but what would be the cost if we didn't take a stand?

"Good Lord," my mom's voice was barely audible. She wiped her nose with her napkin and cleared her throat, "I should call Helen, tonight." Helen was Oly and Charlie's mom. "I'll let her know we will bring dinner over to them tomorrow night."

"A few of us are going over to Charlie's house tonight. I'll let his mom know," Jack said.

My dad looked up and only nodded. I had a feeling he was too choked up to speak. We ate the rest of our dinner listening to the forks and knives clinking on the

Corelle Ware.

My dad was finally able to speak, "Has Mrs. Peters heard any more news about Jesse?" I swallowed the lump in my throat, waiting to hear if mom had spoken to Mrs. Peters. I kept my head down, not wanting to make eye contact. I wasn't great at keeping secrets, especially from my mom and dad.

"No, she hasn't received any new information. Do you think there is anything you can do to find out more about Jesse?"

"I'm not sure if anyone I work with would have access to that information, but I'll give it a try," my dad answered. "By God, that woman needs an answer, that's for sure," he added.

My dad was in the Montana National Guard, and during the 60's and 70's, the Montana Guard's main purpose was to help during state emergencies, like floods and fires. Our soldiers weren't sent to fight in wars, they defended the home front. My brothers would both be joining the National Guard in the upcoming year.

I was dying to tell them that I knew exactly where Jesse was, but I couldn't. I had promised to give Jesse time, but I wasn't sure if I could hold his secret forever. I did feel guilty seeing my parents worry about Jesse and Mrs. Peters, especially after the awful news about Oly Andersen. Hopefully, I would be able to hear the rest of Jesse's story, so I could understand what was going on.

"Dad, do you think the Army is looking for Jesse?" I finally asked.

"I heard that Jesse's unit was in Khe Sanh, and

from what I have seen on the news, our troops were under heavy fire in that area and had to withdraw. Trying to find a missing soldier would be very difficult if the Viet Cong has taken over the area. I would imagine there was quite a bit of chaos and confusion if our troops had to leave under a barrage of artillery fire."

My mom wiped her mouth with her napkin and said, "My God, that poor child."

I suddenly blurted out, "I know-" and stopped abruptly, biting my lip to keep from saying anything else.

"What's that, Betts?" my mom looked at me.

"I know... I know Mrs. Peters must be really sad," I said quickly and looked down at my hands.

"I can't even imagine how it would feel to not know where your child was when you went to bed at night," my mom commented.

We all finished eating without much conversation. When dessert was over, mom reminded Winnie, Roo, and me that it was our turn to do the dishes.

"But I did them last night," I gave her a pleading look.

"Yes, and I made dinner last night, and the night before that, too," my mom tilted her head to me, giving me the look.

"But..."

"Elizabeth Jean, not another word," her voice sounded firm.

Karoline got up and said, "Boy, I'm glad *I* don't have to do ALL of these dishes tonight!" putting a huge emphasis on the word *I* and *ALL*.

"Yeah, thank you, Goober, for doing all of these dishes!" Duke said. "You're going to be up to your neck in suds for hours!"

I grabbed a dish towel and wound it up to make it snap and ran after Duke. I tried to snap him on the behind, but I missed. He turned around and put his hand on my forehead to straight arm me. I of course started swinging at him, hitting only the air between us. He laughed and pushed me back and ran out the door up to Jane's house.

I would keep a mental note of their teasing and get him back later when he was least expecting it. Usually, the best time to make surprise attacks on my brothers, was when they were lying on the carpet watching TV. They would lay on their sides and prop their heads up with their hands, creating a tripod for their heads to rest upon. A perfect scenario for me to come from behind and kick their arms out from under their heads. Watching their surprise as they whacked their heads on the carpeted floor, and yell something like, "What the...?" was priceless. I couldn't linger long to enjoy the moment, because I needed to be out the back door before they could get up on their feet.

I continued to wash the mountain of dishes. "Mom, Jilly and I are going to sleep out in the back yard tonight. It's going to be too hot to be upstairs," I said, as I scrubbed the huge, mashed potato pot.

"Are you asking me or telling me?" she raised her

eyebrow.

"Mom, may we sleep out in the back yard tonight, please?" I restated it as a question.

"I suppose so, but no wandering the neighborhood!" she warned. My mom about had a heart attack late one night when she came out to check on us in the back yard, only to find empty sleeping bags. We had left my yard without telling anyone, to walk to Jilly's garage to get a flashlight. We needed the flashlight to raid Mr. Magoo's raspberry bush because we were hungry. By the time my parents had put their shoes on to come look for us, we were back down the alley with red lips and fingers. They were not happy, not happy at all.

Jilly and I had spent many summer nights in my backyard sleeping under the stars. The six lilac bushes that circled my yard and three apple trees that stood sentry made us feel safe and secure, like a little back yard cocoon. We knew every neighbor in the vicinity which provided extra comfort in the dark Montana night, when our imaginations ran wild.

We set up our sleeping bags and pillows on the grass under the clothesline. Since the streetlights weren't on yet, we still had time to play, so we hurried up to the old high school to see if Jesse could tell us the rest of his story. Our conversation had ended so abruptly; I couldn't stop thinking about it.

We raced up the street, feeling the spray from lawn sprinklers as they shimmered in the glow of the evening sun, highlighting each droplet before falling to the lawns below. Golden beams of sunlight bathed the Cathedral spires above the treetops as if on cue, giving it a heavenly glow. Such a perfectly content scene, worthy of a Bob Morgan masterpiece.

Jilly and I walked clear around Central School to the back side and then cut over to the old high school, just in case anyone was watching us. It would look suspicious if we went straight to the old high school, since every kid in town tried to avoid it at all costs because of the old miner's ghost that haunted it. I started getting creeped out thinking of the ghost.

"I wonder if Jesse has seen the ghost?" Jilly commented, as though she read my mind.

"Maybe he *is* the ghost," I swallowed. Maybe he is the "ghost" that everyone talks about." We both stopped walking and looked at each other.

"Naw, that can't be right. The story of that ghost has been around since the school was built," Jilly surmised.

"Yeah, you're right. Anyways, he looks too human to be a ghost," I said, and we continued walking, "I mean, aren't ghosts transparent and scary looking?"

When we were certain no one was around, including the real ghost, we went near the boarded-up window where Jesse had climbed in. "Jesse," I whispered, "it's Betts and Jilly." After a minute, I could hear the window creak upward and the board scrape across the pebbles lying underneath.

Jesse's eyes squinted and blinked as he tried to adjust to the low angle of the setting sun's rays pointing directly at the window. His hand shook as it shaded his eyes and finally stepped to the side to avoid the glare. He didn't look good. His face seemed pale, and I could see beads of sweat on the sides of his face.

"Are you okay, Jesse? You don't look good," I said, concerned.

"Not feeling great," he turned and sat on the cement floor, with his back leaning against an old wooden desk. "I can't seem to get warm," he crossed his arms across his chest, as though trying to conserve heat, even though the summer evening temperature was still hovering around 80 degrees.

"Oh man, that's not good," Jilly remarked. "Do you need to see a doctor?"

"No, I can't do that," Jesse said quickly, "I'm fine, I just need..." his voice trailed off.

"Chicken soup?" I blurted out. "My mom always gives me chicken noodle soup when I don't feel good. She's a nurse, she knows stuff like that," I said proudly. "Jilly, let's run back to my house, I think we have soup in the basement pantry."

"No, you don't have to do that," Jesse looked up at me and started coughing, "seriously."

"Oh no, I know that" I hesitated, "but if you did want me to tell my parents, I know they could help you, I mean, my mom being a nurse and all," I shrugged.

"I don't think you should tell them you are bringing soup to a soldier who is hiding an old haunted abandoned building, I don't think that would go over too well," he started coughing, wincing with each spasm.

His cough sounded like he was going to hack up a

lung or something. We all winced, it sounded painful.

"Ugh," he closed his eyes and laid his head back against the desk.

"Jesse, we're going to get some soup and I'll see if we have some aspirin or something to help your fever. Is there anything else you need?" I asked.

"No, thank you. You really don't need to do this, I'm not even sure if it will help. I don't want to get anyone into trouble," he worried.

"We will be fine," I assured him, although I knew if Roo was anywhere in the area, it wouldn't be fine. Her nickname being Motormouth, she was like the town crier and made sure everyone knew the goings on in our house and neighborhood. She was better than a guard dog, being that a dog could only bark to warn people, but Roo had an uncanny memory and vocabulary for a six-year-old and could explain everything in great detail.

When we got to my house, I was pleasantly surprised. Roo was at her friend, Lucy's, next door, and the rest of the family was out for the night, except my mom, who was in the living room doing her needlepoint and watching The Smothers Brothers. Dad was there too, but his chair was reclined, and the sound of a buzz saw vibrated from within. I wasn't sure if my mom could hear the TV through the din.

"Betts, is that you?" she asked from the living room when she heard the screen door squeak open.

"Yes, could Jilly and I get an extra blanket from the basement in case we get cold?"

"That's probably a good idea," she said.

I was glad she couldn't see my eyes because she would instantly know that I was lying. She was far better at registering deceit than the lie detector machines on Dragnet. Having practiced her technique on four kids before me, she could have scored a job for the FBI interrogating criminals. The slightest shift in eye movement or uneven breathing would draw her attention, and she was on to the whitest lie or tallest tale.

Jilly and I scampered to the basement and scrounged around our pantry to find some chicken noodle soup. We had a lot of soup, so I doubted my mom would notice one or two missing cans. I grabbed an old blanket to wrap up the soup and ran upstairs.

We needed a can opener, though, and opening the drawer that held the can opener, was like opening a spring trap. There were wire whisks, wooden spoons, beaters, spatulas, spaghetti grabbers, barbecue tools, and any other kitchen utensil you might need to use when you were cooking. Opening that drawer without getting poked in the eye by a flying plastic turkey baster, took skill.

So, when Jilly and I went into the kitchen to get the can opener, I turned on the sink faucet to make noise to muffle the sound of the spring-loaded drawer, and Jilly strategically coughed at the exact moment I tugged on the drawer.

"Jilly, you're not getting sick, are you dear?" my mom yelled from the other room.

We looked at each other with wide eyes, "No, Mrs. Lundberg, I think I just have a tickle. I'm getting some water," and she coughed one more time and guzzled

115

a glass of water. "Much better, thank you!" Jilly called to my mom.

"I'm going to get the aspirin," I mouthed the words to Jilly. She nodded and sat down at the kitchen table. I went into the bathroom and grabbed the aspirin from the cupboard, and quietly shook a few out and folded them into a tissue and put them in the pocket of my jean cut-offs. I went back into the kitchen, "Bye, Mom, we are going to Central to play for a while," I yelled before I closed the back door.

"Okay, watch for the streetlights," she called back.

We hustled up the street to the old high school and checked to make sure the coast was clear of any unwanted visitors. We made our way around back to Jesse's window. I knocked lightly and whispered, "Jesse, it's us."

We could hear Jesse grunt, and the creaking of the wooden desk he was probably using to push himself to a standing position. The window opened, and the wooden board scraped the gravel as he slid it aside.

Dark circles had formed under his sleepy eyes, and my mom would have said he looked peaked. That was the word she always used to describe my tired eyes when I had a cold or the flu. A thought came to my mind that this soup and aspirin was not going to help him get better, but maybe ease his pain. I worried that he probably needed to see a doctor.

"How are you feeling?" I asked him.

"I've been better," his voice was raspy and had that low sound when your chest is full of junk.

"Here's the soup, I wish we could heat it for you," I frowned, "oh, and the aspirin."

"Thank you," and he set it aside. "You really didn't need to do that."

"I don't think you are going to get well if you don't eat, at least that's what my mom always says to me when I'm sick," Jilly said.

"Thank you. Really, thank you for doing all of this for me. I shouldn't have gone to the park today, but I needed to get out of this dark building. I didn't think anyone would notice. I guess I was wrong," he looked up at both of us and a faint smile showed on his face."

"Jesse, do you think you could tell us the rest of the story, if we come back tomorrow?" Jilly asked.

"Yeah, I can do that," he said as he looked both of us in the eyes, "I can do that," he nodded and leaned his head back and closed his eyes. "There's something else I need to explain to both of you, too." He grabbed for his green army jacket that was in his knapsack and covered up with it, with his eyes still closed.

I wondered what else he needed to explain to us, but he looked like he was falling asleep. "See you tomorrow, Jesse," I whispered. The streetlights popped on as Jilly and I stood up to leave. We crossed the street in front of the old high school and started into a run, since that was our cue to be home.

When we got home, we climbed into our sleeping bags. Skip wandered over and assessed the situation, most likely trying to figure out where his sleep spot would be. Finally, he moved toward my feet and spun around several times and plopped down, trapping my toes in place for the night.

Jilly and I watched the sky turn from dark blue to black, revealing star after star, until the whole sky was filled with millions of twinkling lights.

"Betts, are you awake?" Jilly whispered.

"Yeah," I whispered back.

"Do you think Jesse will be okay? I mean, get rid of his sickness for sure, but after that... do you think he will have to go to some military prison or something?"

"I was thinking about that, too," I inhaled deeply and let the air out slowly. "I wish he could have told us the end of that story, maybe he has a good reason for splitting without telling anyone. He doesn't seem like the type that would just give up on service to his country. Yeah," I repeated, "there's no way he would have abandoned his buddies. There's got to be more to his story." I yawned, "Let's go see him first thing in the morning."

CHAPTER 16

As the sun made its way over the treetops, the nest of baby robins in the lilac tree began peeping to let the mama robin know that it was time for their regurgitated worms.

I could hear the loud sound of panting and the smell of warm stinky breath invaded my nostrils. My left eye squinted open to Skip's black shiny nose and drooling tongue, two inches from my face. After noticing my eyes flutter, he licked my face and started frolicking up and down, knowing he would now be getting his breakfast.

"Mornin' Skip," I croaked, eyes blinking to adjust to the morning sun. I scratched behind his ear and he immediately laid down and rolled on his back, so I could give him the same scratching treatment on his stomach.

Jilly and I decided we might as well get up and get on with the day. I didn't like sleeping in, anyways, if the sun was up, so was I. Jilly had to get home to check in with her sisters and eat breakfast.

Inside my house, Roo was at the kitchen table eating her cereal and staring at the back of a Fruity Pebbles box. My whole family knew Roo needed that one bowl of cereal before anyone spoke to her in the morning, otherwise we all would have a very bad day.

My dad was typically at the kitchen table reading the paper as we traipsed into the kitchen, and he was the only one that would venture to speak to Roo before cereal. You could hear his low deep voice, cheerily greet her with, "Good Morning!"

Roo would shuffle through the kitchen in her Strawberry Shortcake nightgown, her wild hair sticking up all over, eyes trying to adjust to the light as she grabbed her Fruity Pebbles and only Fruity Pebbles out of the cereal drawer, each and every day.

"Uhng," she would say in caveman talk, as she poured her cereal in her plastic Lassie bowl, eyes still not quite opened. She would study the back of the cereal box through her sleepy eyes and try to comprehend the amazing facts one could learn from the back of a box of Fruity Pebbles. By the end of the bowl, and maybe an extra helping to sop up the leftover milk, she would come back to life. In observing her nonverbal morning ritual, you would never know she was the one we called Motormouth.

I poured my own bowl of Cap'n Crunch and began to study the maze on the back of the box that the Cap'n needed help in solving, to get to the hidden treasure. There was only so much room on the back of a cereal box, so the maze was easy. The Cap'n should not have needed my help, his sidekick kangaroo could have solved it.

I tried to think about the food I could gather for Jesse. I would have to wait until my parents went to work and Roo was deep into *Romper Room* with Miss Julie before I got things together. Winnie would be waking up soon, so I needed to figure things out before she got involved.

Winnie was a rule follower, and a hard act to follow as far as big sisters go. Winnie was tall and skinny, with long thick hair that hung way down her back. To her own self, she was a geek, but to me, I thought she could have been on the cover of Seventeen magazine. My parents knew if they asked Winnie to help with any chores or other things that kids generally hate to do, she would do it without complaint. It was rare for her to raise her voice or get angry at me, even when I didn't do what she asked me to do. Telling Winnie about hiding a deserter from the US Army was not an option.

I had to act fast before she woke up. I grabbed a large brown Buttery's grocery bag and ran to the basement. I found some chili and a can of Campbell's soup. Back upstairs, I filled an empty milk carton with water. I shoved the supplies in the brown grocery bag and quickly hid it on the back porch and ran upstairs to change out of my pajamas.

Winnie was just coming out of our bedroom. "I'm heading to Jilly's and we're going to Central School for a while," I told her. It wasn't a total lie I just left the part out about Jesse. "I will see you at lunch time," I said, as I looked for my favorite smiley face tee shirt and cut off jean shorts. I quickly changed and tied my moccasins and bounded down the stairs two at a time.

"Bye, Roo!" I poked my head into the living room, but she just raised her hand without looking at me, entranced to Miss Julie's magic mirror on Romper Room.

I grabbed the bag of food and hopped on my orange sting ray bike. I tied the bag to the tall sissy bar in back with one of my jump ropes.

Jilly was already on her bike and waiting for me in the alley. She had made a peanut butter and jelly sandwich. We pedaled quickly up the four blocks to the old high school and brought our bikes to the back, so no one would see them. Jilly knocked on the piece of wood and said quietly, "Jesse, it's Jilly and Betts. Are you there?"

We waited for a minute and then Jilly knocked again, "Jesse, we have some food for you." We heard some movement inside and then a succession of coughs that sounded like a seal barking. He opened the window and struggled to slide the board aside.

He wore his khaki army coat even though it was already 75 degrees. The deep purple circles under his eyes contrasted with his pasty white skin. He looked a bit like a zombie costume I made one Halloween, that required black smudged makeup around my eyes. "Hey," he lifted his hand out of his pocket in a small effort to seem cheerful, eyes squinting from the light.

"I guess you're not feeling much better?" I gave him a worried smile. "Your cough doesn't sound good."

"I'll be okay," he said quietly, "it won't be long."

"It won't be long?" I asked, wondering what he meant.

"I meant, I won't be here long. You know, I can't stay here forever, right?" he looked directly at me. I got a

122

weird feeling, like there was more to say.

I nodded my head and then changed the subject. "Sorry we can't stay longer, we have an errand to run," I told Jesse. Jilly and I had to ride downtown to Union Market to get an order for her mom. Since it was only a few blocks past the school, we left Jesse, and told him we would check on him on our way back.

I glanced at Jilly, "I really want to hear the rest of Jesse's story. How in the heck did he escape Vietnam and come to Helena without someone noticing? I mean, you can't just get on a plane without a ticket. It must have been something so bad that Jesse just freaked out and left for good."

"I know, I'm dying to hear what he has to say," Jilly said, "his grandma would be angry if she knew Jesse was only four blocks away, especially since he is so sick. Betts, do you think we are doing the right thing keeping this from his grandma? I still don't get why he won't tell her he is here."

"I don't know. This is the hardest secret I have ever had to keep. We need to talk to Jesse," I worried.

We parked our bikes in front of the Union Meat Market. It was a small, popular, family-owned meat market. Two of the brothers that owned it, stood behind the counter. "By golly, here come two pretty little ladies, Fred," he winked, and they both smiled at us. "What can we do for you today? How about a freshly made hot dog?" He handed us both a hot dog and Jilly let him know she was picking up an order for her mom. "Oh, by golly, we have that right here, ready to go, little lady! Is there anything else we can get ya?"

Jilly said, "No, that's all, thank you."

"Well, you ladies have a fine day," he smiled and saluted us with flick of his hand. We laughed as we exited the store, finishing the hot dogs. Those guys always made us smile.

I laughed again as I climbed on my bike, "By golly, that hot dog was tasty, little lady."

Jilly mimicked back, "You said it, little lady!" And she saluted me with a flick of her hand.

We were breathless, trying to pedal the steep uphill path from Union Market back to the old high school. It was mid-morning and I already felt the beating rays of the sun on the top of my head. I pictured myself floating in an inner tube in the middle of the bay out at my family's cabin for the up- coming Fourth of July weekend.

At first sight, our cabin was a ramshackle log structure that had wild rabbits living in the fireplace and a greasy car engine sitting on the kitchen table. Ancient, rusted cars were strewn about in the back yard, and the weeds were so tall, we almost lost Roo in them.

The day our parents first introduced us to that old place, we, kids stood and stared at the run-down spectacle before us, thinking our parents had gone mad in wanting to buy it. But one look at the lake view beyond the squalor, and we all fell madly in love with the little red log cabin.

There was much work to do to bring it back to order, but my parents and my aunt and uncle figured with our six kids and their two kids, we would have twelve people working to clean up the place. Everyone had to work until two o'clock in the afternoon painting, mowing,

124

raking, cleaning, pulling weeds and doing various other chores. It didn't matter how old you were either. Even Roo became an expert at digging dandelion roots out of the lawn with a butter knife. My uncle would pay any of us one cent per weed, so Roo was especially interested in earning a quarter for a hard day's work.

When two o'clock came around, rakes, shovels, and butter knives were put away to be replaced with inner tubes and water skis. We would dash to the sandy lake shore and jump in the cool water as though we were on fire. The rest of the afternoon would be spent floating on inner tubes purchased from the Texaco gas station and soaking up the sun on beach towels. The highlight of the day would be skiing behind my uncle's boat, *The Patricia Marie,* named after my Aunt Patricia.

All that hard work provided a feeling of satisfaction each week as we looked at the progress that was made in creating our own Shangri-La on Canyon Ferry Lake. That little piece of heaven would be the glue that held our family together for generations to come. I couldn't wait to get out there.

When Jilly and I arrived back at the school, Jesse was sitting against the building. The sun was beaming down on him, creating a strange golden aura all around him. I thought my eyes were playing tricks on me and I blinked to clear them. Then, when I looked back again at Jesse, everything seemed normal. "Weird," I thought to myself, "that was really weird.

His eyes were closed, and for a split-second I wondered if he was still breathing, until finally, he squinted one eye open. "Hey," he said, which triggered a coughing attack. "I've been so cold, I was having trouble warming up," he cleared his throat.

I smiled back, glad he at least looked like he was back among the living.

"Betts and I are both leaving for the Fourth of July weekend, are you going to be okay until we get back?" Jilly looked concerned."

"I'll be okay," he said, and gave a thumb's up, but the looks on our faces must have been non-believing. He looked at both of us and said seriously, "Everything is going to be okay. I mean that," his voice was shaking. "Now get moving, you have things to do, and so do I," and he began coughing as he lowered himself back through the window.

Before he moved the board back in place, I said, "Bye, Jesse. Take care of yourself." I was a little uneasy as we pedaled away and wondered what things he had to do… and if he really would be okay.

CHAPTER 17

The Fourth of July weekend was supposed to have record breaking temperatures and we kids planned on spending a good portion of our time on inner tubes in the middle of the bay. At night, we would lay in sleeping bags under the stars on the front porch, listening to fish jumping in the bay and looking for satellites orbiting the earth. There was no place any of us would rather be than at that cabin in the summertime.

Winnie, Roo, and I wedged ourselves in to the back seat of our 1968 Plymouth Sedan, between sleeping bags, pillows, and our overnight bags.

Skip jumped on my lap because I had access to the window, and he was obsessed with sticking his head out into the tidal wave of air rushing past our car. When Dad hit 55 miles per hour on the highway, Skip's flapping jowls caused his eyes to close to slits and he appeared to be smiling, which made us laugh, until his flailing tongue sprayed Roo and me with a thick line of slobber. After that, he was reduced to trying to get air out of a three-inch opening in the window that had been rolled up. His snorting black nose lodged into the tiny gap, breathing desperately, as though he was being refused the very air that kept him alive.

When we finally pulled up to the cabin after the half hour drive, Skip bolted from the car and frolicked around as though he had just won the doggy lottery. His first mission was to sniff the trees and woodpile, peeing at each stop. Next, he high tailed it to the lake shore and bounded into the cool clear water, jumping and splashing and barking at the seagulls, who squawked and flapped their wings in effort to get out of his way. We all hesitated in unpacking the car, enamored by the sheer joy of a dog who had finally arrived at his own promised land.

We picked up sticks that had blown into the front and back yards from the surrounding willow trees, so my dad and uncle could mow, without piercing any of our eyes with willow shrapnel that flew from the underside of the mower. A little weed picking in the morning, being it was a holiday weekend, and we would be able to spend the rest of the time playing in the lake and exploring the hills with our cousins who were coming from Great Falls.

Our Aunt Sarah and Uncle George, along with their five kids surprised us and arrived before noon the next morning. Getting a family of seven up-and-at-'em before noon, packed and ready for a two-and-a-half-hour road trip, was a feat of organized precision. My Uncle George honked the horn to announce their arrival, as their wood paneled station wagon left a dust cloud in its trail on the rutted road that ended at our cabin. Four doors flew open as soon as the car stopped, and five kids burst out of the hot car, shouting and waving hello, as though they were spring-loaded from inside.

We helped to unload the mountain of supplies

they had packed in preparation for the long weekend. It reminded me of those clown cars at the circus, where clowns just kept coming out of the tiny car, and you could never figure out how they had all fit inside such a tiny space. Sleeping bags, suitcases, groceries, and other goods kept coming out of the station wagon, as we made trip after trip from car to cabin. How in the heck did seven people also fit inside that vehicle? It was a mystery in my mind that would never be solved.

All of us kids changed into our suits, grabbed towels and inner tubes and made a dash for the lake. Our dads settled in by the horseshoe pits while the moms started preparing for dinner, which was the usual huge spread of food designed to fill up the hungriest of children after a day of swimming.

The two boys, Jeffy, who was eleven, and Joe, nine, threw their towels on the beach and raced into the cold lake water, whooping and hollering about the shock of coldness hitting their skin. We girls on the other hand, laid our towels down to gather warmth from the sun and work on our tans, with baby oil and Hawaiian Tropics being in high demand.

"Ahhh, this is livin' people," I smiled, and stretched out on my Partridge Family beach towel, between Winnie and Roo. Roo was wearing a two-piece suit that had a little skirt attached to the bottoms. Mom had bought her a pair of sunglasses that had yellow duckies attached on each side, and a sailor hat with the words "Summer Fun!" written on the front.

Roo didn't get much sleep the night before. But, when she did doze off, she slept hard. As she stumbled out of her sleeping bag in the morning, her Smurf blue cheek matched her Smurf blue sleeping bag, after having been drooled on all night long.

She had only been lying on her towel for a couple of minutes, sunglasses covering her eyes, hat low on her forehead, when I heard a low rumble come from her direction. Skip, who was lying on my towel, looked up and cocked his head, confused about the source of the sound. Roo was sound asleep, drool already seeping from the side of her mouth, with another rumble from deep within, beginning to erupt. Skip cocked his head the other way, still wondering where that noise was coming from. We all laughed, wondering how such a tiny human could make such a ruckus.

It wasn't ten minutes later when I noticed a suspicious quietness, even Roo had rolled over and stopped snoring. The boys weren't making noise anymore which meant they had either drowned, or they were up to no good. I decided the latter was most likely and I squinted one eye open to make a quick sweep of the water in front of me. Out of my peripheral vision, I noticed a movement and lifted my head, then opened the other eye to fully investigate.

"Look out, Jamie!" I yelled to my cousin on the far end of the line of towels, but it was too late. Her two brothers had a huge bucket of water balancing over her head, strands of green slimy seaweed dangling off the handle. Before I could get the words out to warn her, they had flung the water, not only on Jamie, but across the whole line of six girls lying on the beach.

"AAHHHH!" We yelled at the shock of ice water hitting our baking skin.

"Whaaaa!" Roo began to cry from the surprise of being awoken from her slumber.

"You guys wait! Just wait, until you're least expecting it!" Jamie, who was the eldest sister at fourteen, yelled at her brothers, who were now laughing and jumping back into the water.

"Yeah," I chimed in, "like when you are sleeping all snug and cozy in your sleeping bag tonight!" We all laughed.

"Yeah," Roo sniffed, "you will cry for your mama and probably wet the bed!" We all laughed harder, and then Roo looked around and started to laugh because we were all laughing.

We spent the rest of the afternoon floating on inner tubes and competing in diving contests from the dock. My Uncle Paddy pulled us skiing behind the Patricia Marie. He pulled me way around Cemetery Island, which was indeed a graveyard on an island, in the middle of the lake.

The area had been home to the Blackfeet people a century before, but, as the bison disappeared and the U.S. government went back on their word, the tribe was forced to relocate to reservation land near Glacier Park in 1888. Settlers slowly began to enter the area.

Canyon Ferry Lake was created in the 1950's when they built a dam across a narrow strip of the Missouri River, about twenty miles north west of Helena. Lots of homesteads, farms, and a small town were flooded, so the surrounding area could have access to hydroelectric power. People in the farming community had no choice but to sell the land that had been in their families for generations.

When the lake was formed, a decision was made to leave the local cemetery where it was established, and not relocate it. The cemetery had been there since the 1870's, and there it would stay as an island, in the middle of a popular recreational area for boaters and fishermen.

Of course, we had scary campfire stories since there was a creepy cemetery within view of our cabin. That night, as we, kids roasted marshmallows around the campfire near the beach, my eleven-year-old cousin, Jeffy, retold a traditional campfire tale. It concerned a recluse who went out on the lake, on a dark cloudy night in his small wooden rowboat, and things went awry. Of course, we had all heard the story many times, but we never tired of hearing it again. This time it would be Jeffy's version.

Jeffy's voice lowered to a dramatic whisper, and his eyes, semi-covered with his brown shaggy bangs, were opened wide as he looked each one of us in the eye, through the flickering of the fire. "The year they flooded this land," he moved his arm in a sweeping motion toward the lake, "people were mad as hell!" He smacked his fist into the palm of his hand.

We all looked at each other and snickered at his use of a forbidden swear word. Roo's eyes, of course darted between Winnie's and mine as she let out a gasp and covered her mouth in shock. "Yes, I said mad as hell, because the government had taken their land right out from under them," he hissed, and spit into the fire.

He looked back up and paused, I swallowed a gulp of air. "One of those angry landowners was an old, old man, hair white as snow and a beard that hung to his chest, who had lived on this land as a baby, before they even had cars.

Well, one night, the old man began to paddle his rickety wooden boat across the lake, to make his nightly visit to his beloved wife's grave on Cemetery Island. The boat was old and less than seaworthy, and it took great effort for him to paddle across the lake on this particular night, because there was a storm brewing over the mountain." Our eyes followed in the direction he pointed to across the lake at the mountains beyond Yacht Basin Marina.

"But he didn't care about no storm. He visited Ginnie, his true love, every night, and this night would be no different. He kept rowing with all his might, against the wind as waves began to crash against the hull of his boat," he slapped his legs for effect, "and rain soaked through his clothes. The rowboat began to take on water, still, he rowed and rowed and rowed!" Jeffy's voice grew louder. "Lightning flashed left and right, right and left," he made his fingers burst open left and right and back again. "He wouldn't give up and pulled with all of his might against the wind. Water had gushed into the boat and had risen as high as the seats and kept rising and rising and rising. Finally, the little boat could not stay afloat any longer and just like that," he snapped his fingers, "it sank like a stone to the bottom of the lake."

"The old man could not swim but was wearing an orange life vest that kept him afloat as the storm raged around him. He bounced and bobbed violently, Cemetery Island just yards away. So close, and yet, so far," Jeffy shook his head, and breathed in deeply. "He just couldn't get there," Jeffy said softly, voice cracking, and held his palms upward to let them drop heavily on his lap.

Everyone was entranced with Jeffy's storytelling, eyes wide, riveted with each word, even though they had heard it ten times before.

"Suddenly!" Jeffy's voice shouted, and we all jumped. "Suddenly, a boat full of teenagers, who were racing home through the storm on the black moonless night, blinded from the rain, accidentally hit the old man's boat from behind!" Jeffy clapped his hands loudly.

"He didn't even see it coming," he shook his head sadly. "The boat had been pounding through the whitecaps, so the kids believed they had hit a piece of wood or debris loosened from the storm. The boat had in fact, ran its length over the old man, ending with the propeller slicing through his head," Jeffy made a slicing motion across the side of his head, "knocking him unconscious." At this mention, Roo was now covering her eyes with her hands.

"He floated in the lake through the night," Jeffy continued, "half of his head missing in the murky green water. Hours and hours, he floated, giant carp circling and circling," Jeffy twirled his pointer finger around and around, "waiting for his demise.

By sunrise the next morning, he had somehow washed upon the shore of Cemetery Island, half alive," and he barely whispered, "with barely half of a head." Roo was now sitting in Winnie's lap, holding her ears and burying her eyes in Winnie's shoulder.

Jeffy continued in a whisper, "The old man wouldn't give up though, he just had to see his wife. He began to crawl, inch by inch up the hill toward his beloved's grave," Jeffy pantomimed a clawing motion with his hands, "blood squirting out of the half of his head that was still attached. But try as he might, he-just-couldn't-do-

134

it." For dramatic effect, he repeated himself in a barely audible whisper, "he just… could… not… do… it. There he lay… dead, half of a head, only yards from his wife's grave. He would never get to say goodbye to his beloved Ginnie."

"Now, to this day, Half Head haunts this lake, looking for his wife. Even worse, he roams the lake vowing revenge on the teenagers who kept him from his beloved Ginnie.

So, beware! On the darkest of nights, when you can't see your hand in front of your face and when the moon gives no reflection off the lake, you will hear the moaning of Half Head as he searches for the teenagers who took his life. Wher-r-r-e ar-r-re they-y-y?" Jeffy moaned and looked around the group in a zombie-like trance.

We were silent as he kept repeating the words until suddenly, "IS IT YOU!" he shouted and grabbed Winnie who was sitting next to him.

"SHIT!" she yelled and pushed Jeffy off the log he was perched upon. He laughed, but she looked mortified at her sudden use of a swear word and covered her mouth. We all burst out laughing, especially me, because that was the first time I had ever heard Winnie say a bad word.

"That story is so creepy," I shook my hands as though I was flinging the evil spirits off them. It seemed like with each telling of the Half Head legend, details were embellished and became a little more gruesome. The original story didn't even involve half of a head, it had been a gash that took off the old man's right ear.

Right then, a noise at the edge of the water caught

135

our attention, and the laughter immediately ceased, until Winnie noticed it was only a piece of driftwood lapping against the boat. We all sat there looking at each other, for fear of breaking the silence and giving away our location to Half Head. I looked at the fire slowly burning out, and glanced at the sky, thankful to see the full moon reflecting off the water.

Right then, Duke burst out of nearby bushes, yelling, "Half Head is here! I'm coming to get you! Wooo-oooo!"

We screamed bloody murder and started running for the safety of the cabin, even though we knew it was Duke trying to scare us. Duke's laughter was joined by Jack's, and two of his friends who had just arrived.

Duke yelled, "Goobie, your turn to shut off the sprinklers!"

"No way!" I yelled back. "You do it!" But I knew there was no getting out of it.

The shut-off valve was located inside an old pump house, a shack type structure that needed repair but contained the water pump for our cabin. It was super scary going back there because of the darkness and seemed to be a world away from the noise and ruckus of people on the other side of the cabin. Besides, it seemed like an ideal place for Half Head to hide out.

I drew the short straw on this night. After listening to Jeffy's dramatic interpretation of Half Head's demise, I was spooked. But Duke and Jack were still down near the beach, so the chances of them trying to scare me was slim.

I took a deep breath and started toward the first dark corner of the cabin. Tiptoeing, to make the least amount of noise possible, I prayed I wouldn't step on a dried twig or something and make noise. Approaching the corner, the music faded away and my thumping heart kept time with the rhythm of the pump. It would be a mad sprint for the turn-off valve because I knew, I absolutely knew, it was inevitable that someone would be hiding in wait to jump out and scare the crap out of me.

"One-two-three," I counted, and bolted toward the shed. The wet grass made it easy to use a softball slide the last ten feet, to quickly reach the turn-off valve. I twisted the knob as fast as I could to turn it off. "Righty tighty, lefty loosey, righty tighty, left loosey," I kept repeating in my head. "Hurry up, hurry up," I muttered, and felt the urge to pee.

Mission completed, the sprinkler's "chicka, chicka" was silenced and I jumped up to head back to the light.

Little did I know, or maybe I did know, my mischievous Aunt Sarah, who was a 40-year-old teenager, and a mother of five, who could never resist a good practical joke, was hiding in wait. She jumped from behind the shed and cackled like the wicked witch in the Wizard of Oz.

My high-pitched scream reached the other side of the cabin, and immediate laughter echoed across the lake. I scampered back to the light and the lawn chair circle of smiling people. Nothing else to do but join in and laugh it off, while shaking my head in disbelief that I had been duped by the sprinkler patrol once again.

CHAPTER 18

Monday morning came and Jilly and I, both tired from the long Fourth of July weekends at our family cabins, coasted to Memorial Park to the sound of bike tires on black top. We caught up with our baton class in the band shell and ran to take our places.

The theme song from *Hawaii 5-0* echoed across the park as we marched and performed butterflies and pancakes accompanied by kick ball changes. Our teacher kept time, "One, two, three, kick, five, six, seven ball change. Butterfly, two, three, four, again, six, seven, eight. Looking good, ladies! We only have a few days until the Kiddie's Parade, so let's try it again," she looked back at us while placing the needle to the 45 back at the beginning of the record.

I didn't mind all the practice. I would do it a hundred times more, if that is what it took to be part of the Kiddie's Parade during Stampede Week in our town. The Boy Scouts would lead the parade. Behind them, miniature versions of cowboys, ranchers, farmers, clowns, Native Americans, and twirlers would smile and wave as they paraded down Last Chance Gulch. Parents and shop owners would line the streets, clapping and waving American flags as we went by them. An example of small-town America at its finest.

Just as we were finishing the finale, I heard Winnie's faint voice calling my name. I turned to scan the perimeter of the park, shading my eyes with my hand. I spotted Winnie flying across the grass on her ten-speed bike.

"Betts! Betts! Is Roo with you?" she slammed on her brakes and skidded across the grass, breathless as she tried to get the words out again. "Is Roo…," she panted, "is Roo with you?" The frightened look in her eyes told me this was serious.

"No, I haven't seen her!" I jumped off the band shell stage two steps at a time. "Is she at Lucy's? She's probably at Lucy's!" I tapped on the sides of my legs, trying to think of the places Roo liked to go.

That was not the first time Roo had disappeared. When she was four, my parents took us to the Stampede Fair and Carnival. Roo eyed the Zipper, which was a stomach-churning ride meant for screaming teenagers and daredevils alike. Each cage would spin on its own axle as the entire ride went up and down and around. Items that weren't secured, such as coins in pockets and people's upchucked corn dogs and funnel cakes, would fly through the air and land on the spectators below.

Roo had spotted the bright lights before we were even out of the car. "I want to go on that one!" she grinned, pointing, as if in a zombie-like trance.

My mom only smiled, thinking she would change her mind when she saw the little kids' airplane ride.

"Let's go on that BIG ride!" she squealed again. My parents' eyes locked, eyebrows raised, knowing Roo was not going to let this rest.

"Roo, they have airplane rides that fly you through the air! Wouldn't that be fun?" Winnie said, trying to sound excited. "Besides, you have to be this tall to ride The Zipper," and she held her hand up above Roo's head.

Roo frowned and said, "Nuh-uh. That's not true, is it Betts," she looked at me.

"Sorry, Roo, maybe next year you'll be tall enough, besides, didn't you just eat a sloppy Joe for dinner? Do you know what that would look like coming back up?" I shook my head and pantomimed barfing in my hand. "Not good. The ride operators would not like that at all. You'd probably be banned from the Zipper for life. You don't want that to happen, do you?"

She managed the tiniest shake of her head and crossed her arms over her chest. Thinking it had been settled, my mom took her place in the long ticket line, while my dad stood in the shade of the Ferris Wheel talking to someone. Winnie and I motioned to Dad, to let him know we were going to walk around while we waited for our tickets.

As we walked, I kept looking back at the ticket line to see if my mom was making progress. Finally, I noticed she was at the ticket window, so Winnie and I made our way back to them. Mom handed Winnie and I some tickets. We were about to take off for the Zipper when she asked, "Where's Roo?"

"I dunno? I thought she was with you," Winnie looked around at mom.

140

All three of us instinctively looked for my dad, who was still standing in the shade of the Ferris Wheel in deep conversation. But when he felt our eyes boring holes in him, he looked up and saw the blank expressions on all our faces.

"Is Roo with you?" my mom's eyes were begging him to say yes. But the look on his face confirmed her fear. My heart sank, wondering how we could find her in the crowded carnival.

"I thought she was..." he began, "don't panic," my dad held up his hands, "she couldn't have gotten far, I'm sure she's nearby. Betts and Winnie, sweep through the game area, I'll check the rides."

"I'll stay in this area in case she comes back here," my mom said, all the while her eyes scanning every nook and cranny she could see from that spot. "Hurry, please!"

We all took off. Winnie and I ran frantically through the game area, asking people if they had seen a six-year-old, pig-tailed girl in bib overalls. Minutes ticked by as each person shook their head, no. "What if she's been kidnapped?" I whispered to Winnie.

"Don't," she stopped, "don't even say that."

I tried not to think about it, as we made a full circle around the game area. But, in a split second, it dawned on me, "I think I know where she is," I said as we approached my mom.

"Where?" they both looked at me.

As if we all read each other's minds, we agreed simultaneously, "Zipper!"

Yes, Roo had almost made her way to the front of the Zipper line. Easy to spot since she was the shortest one there. Roo didn't argue when my parents scooped her up. I think she was secretly glad they had found her. The towering ride was much more intimidating up close.

This time, I was trying to think like Roo, and of places only she would go. "Are you sure she's not at Lucy's?"

"No, they went to Yellowstone," Winnie reminded me. "Where's your bike, let's get home... hurry!"

Jilly and I both followed Winnie on our bikes and pedaled the uphill route to our house, the fastest we had ever done. My legs were burning, but I didn't stop until we reached home.

"Roo!" I began yelling. "Roo!"

Jilly rode up the street and Winnie scoured the house again, to make sure Roo hadn't returned while she was gone. I looked in our back yard under the lilacs and beneath the back porch, where we had a small fort.

Winnie ran out front again and began to yell, a little louder with more urgency, "Roo! Where are you? ROO!"

That's when Mrs. Peters came shuffling from her backyard, quicker than her usual gait, holding Roo's hand, the other hand waving her hankie at Winnie. "Young lady, are you looking for your little girl? Young lady..." she waved her handkerchief at Winnie.

Winnie answered, "Yes! Roo, where have you been? We have been looking all over for you!"

Winnie ran across the street to Mrs. Peters' yard and knelt to hug a confused Roo, who asked, "What's wrong?"

I ran across the street to join them.

"What's wrong? What's wrong? We have been looking for you for fifteen minutes, that's what's wrong! You scared the heck out of me!" Winnie finally let go and stood up.

"I'm sorry, dearie, she wandered into my backyard and told me you had left on your bike. She couldn't find anyone. I told her she could stay and have some lemonade with me, that I was sure you would be right back," Mrs. Peters explained.

"Roo, why didn't you answer when I was calling you the first time?" Winnie asked her.

Roo looked down at her feet, "I just went out of the back yard for a minute..." She looked up, "Are you mad at me?"

"No, I'm not mad," Winnie's voice softened, "but you really scared me. You can't just leave the yard and not tell anyone." Winnie looked at Mrs. Peters, "Thank you, Mrs. Peters, that was very kind of you. Roo, what do you say to Mrs. Peters?"

Roo reached for Winnie's hand and tucked her chin to her chest. Her eyes raised to meet Mrs. Peters' smile and she uttered a shy, "Thank you, Mrs. Peters."

"You are welcome, dear," she smiled warmly, which may have been the first time I had ever seen Mrs. Peters smile. "I haven't had visitors for a long time. My grandson, Jesse, use to sit and have lemonade with me on these warm summer days. I miss that," her hand went up to touch a locket hanging by a delicate chain around her neck. I guessed a picture of Jesse was inside it, and maybe a picture of her son, Jesse's dad, alongside it.

"Well, thanks again," Winnie said as she grabbed Roo's hand.

We started walking across the street. I glanced back at Mrs. Peters, thinking she would go back in her house, but she stood there. I had the feeling she wanted us to stay, even though she still didn't know our names.

"She's not as mean as she looks," Roo said happily, while hopping onto a kitchen chair. I grabbed a can of tomato soup to heat up for lunch and Winnie started making grilled cheese sandwiches. Roo went on, "She's just sad she can't find her son," she laid her chin on her arms that were crossed on top of the kitchen table and watched me open the soup, her expression changing to a frown.

I turned to look at Winnie and then to Roo, "She told you that?" I was surprised Mrs. Peters would divulge such a topic to a six-year-old.

"Yeah, but he's not lost," Roo reached down to tie her shoelace. Lynn and I exchanged confused looks.

"What?" I half laughed. "What would make you say that?"

"Because I talked to him, silly," Roo laughed.

"What are you talking about, Roo? He is in Vietnam. He is missing in action," I stared at her, forgetting about the soup heating on the stove.

"Nuh uh," she shook her head.

"Roo, where exactly did you see him?" Winnie asked.

"When I couldn't find you anywhere, I ran out of the house and I started yelling for you..." her voice grew soft, "and I was crying, because I was scared nobody was here. So, I ran to the triangle park, and was just sitting on the swing and crying, and then Jesse told me to go to Mrs. Peters' house. So, I did."

"Jesse Peters? Jesse was at the park?" Winnie asked.

"He was sitting near the tree, and then he wasn't," she shrugged her shoulders.

"What do you mean?" I was more confused.

"Well, I heard him say my name, and I looked up and saw him," and her voice grew deeper...

"Roo, go to my grandma's house. She will help you." But when I looked by the tree where the voice came from, nobody was there," Roo rested her chin in her hands. "I think it was Jesse."

"What the...?" I put my hands on my head. "How would you know it was Jesse?"

"I don't know, he was wearing army clothes like the guys on the news," she shrugged her shoulders again, "and he said to go to his grandma's house."

"Were you scared?" I sat down on the chair next

145

to her.

"No, I wasn't afraid, I just got off the swing and went to Mrs. Peters' house." Then Roo changed the subject, "is lunch almost done? I'm hungry."

I looked at the bubbling tomato soup on the stove and knew that pan would need a soaking when it came time to clean up. I grabbed three bowls and started dishing the soup into them. Winnie cut the grilled cheese sandwiches in half and put them on plates.

We sat down, not sure what to make of Roo's story. Roo was known to stretch the truth at times, mainly to avoid getting into trouble, but she seemed sincere in her recollection. If what she said was true, I wanted to find Jesse. Jilly and I hadn't seen him since before the Fourth of July weekend, and I wondered what he had been doing all that time. I looked at Winnie, debating whether I should tell her that I had also seen Jesse.

Winnie dipped her sandwich into her tomato soup and saw me staring at her, as she lifted her head to take a bite. "What?" she frowned.

I was in deep thought and didn't realize I was staring at her. "Nothing," I grabbed my soup spoon and started to eat. After a few bites I blurted out, "I've seen Jesse, too," and looked up to see Winnie's reaction.

Her eyes were non-believing, "Yeah, right."

"I'm not kidding. He's been hiding out in the old high school, next to Central. Jilly and I talked to him," I said.

"No way, you're lying," she shook her head. "Why

would he be staying in a creepy old building, and not at his grandma's house? That just doesn't make sense," she shook her head and dunked her sandwich in the soup.

"I know, that's what we thought, too. Jesse doesn't want us to tell his grandma that he is here, but he looked really bad the last time we saw him... he was coughing and had the chills, and was pasty white," I bit my lip, "and we were trying to decide if we should tell someone, so he could get help. He also started to tell Jilly and I how his unit came under attack, but we were never able to hear the end of the story."

Winnie's eyes were wide as I relayed the story. "No way," she shook her head. "There is absolutely no way that Jesse is hiding out. That would mean he is AWOL, and he could be sent to military prison, or something like that." She shook her head in disbelief, and then as if she'd changed her mind, "Are you positive it's him?"

"Let's go to Central after lunch and I will show you," I said, as I sopped up the remaining soup with my grilled cheese.

We finished our lunch and cleaned up the kitchen. I wished Jilly could have come with Winnie and me, but she had a dentist appointment. Roo was going to have to come with us because we didn't have any other options. "Roo, if you come with us, you have to promise you won't tell *anyone*!" I said.

"I won't! I promise!" she smiled at me with her hands clasped tightly under her chin.

"Cross your heart, hope to die, stick a needle in your eye?" I said with my hands on my hips.

"Betts, I don't want a needle in my eye," her eyes were wide.

"Well, then don't tell anyone, okay?" I said.

"I won't, I promise! I never want a needle in my eye!" Her hands were both on the sides of her eyes like blinders on a racehorse, as though she was shielding her eyes from any needles flying haphazardly through the air.

"Okay, I am trusting you to keep this a secret. Let's get going," I started for the front door.

Winnie, Roo, and I rode our bikes the four blocks to Central School and parked in the back, so they were out of sight.

Gray clouds, heavy with moisture, rumbled above our heads, causing the old school to look more haunted than normal. Winnie's long hair began whipping into her face and we held up our hands to protect our eyes from the top layer of sand blowing off the Battlefield. Roo grabbed Winnie's hand and moved in closer to her.

"We should hurry," Winnie shouted through the wind, "it looks like it's going to rain."

I led them to the boarded window that Jesse used to get in and out of the building. "Right here," I pointed, and proceeded to knock on the board. "Jesse, it's Betts," I cupped my mouth, so he could hear me through the wind. There was no answer. "Jesse?" I kept knocking.

The wind was blustering around us and I hastily slid the board away from the opening, not waiting for an answer and scanned the abandoned classroom, but Jesse was nowhere in sight. In fact, it didn't look like anyone, or anything had been inside for a long time, judging by the untouched dust coating the floor and desks.

"What the...?" I looked around, confused by the lack of human existence. "Where...?" I leaned in closer, looking at the desk where I had seen Jesse sitting against the last time I had talked to him.

Winnie saw my confusion. "Do we have the right room? Are you sure this is where Jesse was staying?" she asked.

"Where did he go?" Roo asked.

"I'm not sure," I answered. "This is where Jilly and I saw him. I'm positive. I just don't get it; it doesn't even look like anyone has been in here."

Suddenly a big thunder boomer sounded, and we all jumped. Rain began pouring out of the sky and Winnie and Roo rushed inside the room with me. We turned to see water drenching The Battlefield. It was coming down hard and there was no way we would be leaving anytime soon.

"It's scary in here," Roo whispered, looking around at the dusty desks that cluttered the room. The chalkboard up front still had a math lesson on it, as though the students had just gotten up and walked out, never to have returned. A framed picture of a young George Washington hung tilted on the wall, next to a dusty American flag near the front of the room.

There were old math books stacked on shelves next to a faded black and white photograph of Albert Einstein, sitting with his hands clasped in front of him. Next to Einstein, was some guy with with long hair, who could possibly have been a member of *The Doobie Brothers*, but the nameplate below the picture said, "Isaac Newton" and I didn't remember anyone named Isaac Newton being a member of *The Doobie Brothers*.

Another round of thunder and lightning lit up the air. "We aren't going to be able to leave until the storm lets up," I whispered, trying not to disrupt anything or anyone that might have heard us enter the building.

We sat there close to twenty minutes watching the rain splash onto the dirt. Eyes level with the playground, I followed the trails of little rivers that were racing down toward The Battlefield, creating a series of mini lakes. If school was in session, the brand-new water features on The Battlefield would be like magnets to kids let out for recess. What kid could resist the chance to play in a puddle? Rainy days meant running next to homemade stick boats as they rushed down the street gutters or collecting worms that had taken refuge on the sidewalks, but in this storm, we would be human lightning bolts out on the empty Battlefield.

"This storm isn't going to let up anytime soon, let's go look around," Winnie whispered.

Roo had been staring at the picture of the guy from *The Doobie Brothers*. "No-o-o," she looked up at Winnie, and clamped on to her arm with both hands. I was with Roo. I didn't really want to look around in a building that was creepy enough to be part of *Psycho's* movie set.

"You guys wait here, then," Winnie said, "I want to look around. Roo and I looked at each other and moved closer to Winnie who had begun to walk toward the classroom door. We were so close to Winnie's back, that we gave her shoe a flat tire, and she had to bend down to dig out the heel of her shoe.

It was dark in the hallway and Roo's hand found its way into mine. We each walked as though we were stepping on eggshells, eyes wide, on the lookout for the ghosts and spirits that had been part of school playground lore for decades. Dust particles woke up and bounced in the tiny streams of light escaping from cracks in the boarded windows. Strewn papers beneath lockers and bulletin boards lining the hallway, gently fluttered in our wake.

Suddenly, a loud "BANG!" almost made me lose my lunch! We stopped as though our feet were nailed down to the floor. Our screams in perfect unison, we clung together purely by reflex. I opened my eyes to look down the hallway for the source of the commotion. Fluttering papers were settling to the floor, and my heart was beating out of my chest. We stood, glued together, afraid to move, afraid to make a sound. We waited, and I prayed thinking, hoping, it was Jesse making the noise.

"Wait a minute," Winnie broke the silence, "guys, it's just the wind from the storm. I'll bet it blew the board against the broken window."

I heard the noise again and felt another gust of wind. More papers fluttered. I realized that Winnie's conclusion made sense, thank the Lord. At least that was what I had decided to believe, to make myself think we weren't about to be murdered by the ghost of a crusty old miner.

I finally let loose of Winnie and heard Roo exhale. "Holy shit!" she breathed, hands holding onto her head as if it were going to explode. Winnie and I stared at her, trying to absorb this new phrase that Roo had chosen to use. We burst out laughing, our voices echoing down the cavernous hallway, releasing the nervous tension. Neither Winnie nor I, opted to give Roo a lecture on her interesting use of the English language, because our own thought bubbles were an exact copy of Roo's.

We kept making our way down the hallway, eyes darting from side to side, on guard and hyper-sensitive. Beams of light were filtering in through a row of small windows, as we came upon an unexpected sight. Four huge stone pillars stood solidly to the left of us. The pillars seemed out of place, perhaps belonging in the Greek Acropolis, where Caesar would have spoken to his council, not in an abandoned high school in Helena, Montana. The pillars themselves had ornate cornices at the top near the ceiling and on the other end near the floor. A maze-like design wrapped around the middle of each pillar, reminding me of a design on the Coliseum I'd seen, in a book about Greek mythology. The pillars divided intricate archways made of bricks, that looked as though someone had spent a great deal of time creating such work.

"What is this place?" Roo's voice echoed.

"It looks like the grand entrance of the school," Winnie examined in awe.

"It's pretty," Roo smiled as she looked all around. It's like Cinderella's castle."

"This is so cool," I whispered, my eyes moving upward examining each detail. "I don't get why this school was abandoned. What a waste of a cool place," I frowned.

"I agree," Winnie said. It stinks we will never be

able to share this. We would be in big trouble if anyone knew we were inside, right, Roo?" Winnie reminded her.

"I won't tell!" Roo replied as she studied the pillars.

I imagined in the late 1890's when it was built, high school students in their long dresses and collared shirts and ties, running up the stairs, so they were not late to class, hands grasping onto the pillars as they turned to enter the staircase. Their voices echoing through the archways talking about the upcoming football game or homecoming dance. Wouldn't they find it amusing seeing the three of us in our cut-off shorts and t-shirts standing in their hallway sixty years later? They would most likely be aghast at our clothing choices.

The storm stopped as quickly as it had started, and now bright sunlight streamed onto our faces through small windows where the wall met the ceiling. I expected harp music or trumpets to sound out, like in the movies, when the hero comes upon a long-lost gold mine, lit by a ray of light from above to make the gold sparkle. I felt as though we had found a hidden treasure, and it was just blocks from our house.

We were jolted out of our trance by Roo. "Winnie, I have to go to the bathroom," Roo began to cross and uncross her legs.

"Yeah, we should probably go," she said, but like me, Winnie wanted to linger, imagining what this old high school would've looked like back in its glory days. "C'mon, let's go," and she nudged me back down the hallway.

I had almost forgotten our reason for going to the old high school in the first place, and remembered we were looking for Jesse, as we exited through the broken window of the classroom. As we drove our bikes off the rain-soaked Battlefield, I looked around, and hoped Jesse didn't get caught out in the open during the storm. I wondered where he was. It was strange how we couldn't find any traces of him being in the classroom.

CHAPTER 19

When my parents found out about Roo going missing, and taking refuge at Mrs. Peters' house, she got a talking to, and had to write a thank you note to Mrs. Peters and invite her to our house for dinner. Roo also had to set the dining room table, which only got used for special occasions or when guests came to dinner.

I personally wasn't excited about Mrs. Peters coming to our house, after all, she was the crankiest lady in the neighborhood. I told my mom that Roo should be the one to sit next to her since they were apparently good friends, now. My mom raised an eyebrow at that statement.

Pot roast was a popular dinner in our house, so that meant Karoline, Jack, and Duke were in attendance. Mrs. Peters was introduced to all of us, and I wondered if she would remember our names the next day. She sat between Roo and my dad. She seemed to be surprised at the amount of food, especially considering my mom had spent the last eight hours working at the hospital.

When my dad asked Mrs. Peters where she had

grown up, she smiled wide enough for me to see her false teeth. She shared a few stories of growing up on her family farm on the Hi-Line, in northern Montana.

She laughed about sneaking up on some boys who were skinny-dipping in a nearby swimming hole one hot summer afternoon, when she was twelve years old. She and a couple friends came upon them and stole their clothes and hung them on the fence posts that lined a nearby road.

"Oh, you should have seen their faces as they were looking for their britches," her hands pressed to her cheeks as though she was recalling their embarrassment. Her head tilted back in laughter. "When those boys finally noticed a pair of underwear hanging on the barb wire near the road, they skittered so fast to grab the rest of their clothes, they were tripping and falling..." she stopped and laughed again, which made all of us laugh, "and who do you think drove by right as they made it to the road? None other than the new pastor himself! Oh my, you should have heard the sermon that next Sunday morning!" Her hands flattened onto her chest as she recalled the moment, "Good Lord, I have never heard such fire and brimstone!"

We all laughed, and maybe I laughed the hardest, thinking Mrs. Peters sounded like she would have been fun to have as a friend in her younger years. Mrs. Peters transformed into a different person as she shared her childhood with all of us. I looked around the table at each member of my family and they were genuinely engaged in every word Mrs. Peters spoke. Usually when old people rambled on about the past, I zoned out into unconsciousness. But we had caught a small glimpse of Mrs. Peters' world that evening, and she wasn't as mean as I thought. She had been such a stranger for these past few years, even though she lived a mere forty steps from our front door.

Later that evening, my mom reminded me, "Everyone has a story to tell, especially the elderly. We just need to take the time to listen and get to know them." I thought, Mrs. Peters was a regular person once, but life's disappointments caused her to lose herself.

Roo, Winnie, and I did the dishes that night while my mom and dad visited with Mrs. Peters. Karoline, Jack, and Duke of course had pressing engagements with their friends, and took off right after dinner.

My mom pulled Karoline aside and asked her to stay away from the demonstrations at the Capitol. People had been protesting the Vietnam War all over the country, and there were rumors about a gathering at the Capitol building this night. Karoline wasn't really a protester, but two of her friends attending college at Berkeley had been arrested for participating at a sit-in, and Karoline was curious about all of it. She knew my dad would not want to see his daughter protesting this war, but Karoline had just turned twenty-one, and she was an adult.

I understood how my dad felt about protesters. A few nights earlier, we had watched the news on our console TV, as Walter Cronkite interviewed John Lennon lookalikes and Janis Joplin wannabes, who were demonstrating at the Los Angeles International Airport. In the background, the two shoe-less Janis Joplins, who didn't look much older than Winnie, had peace signs painted on their faces, and bell-bottoms that splashed every color in the rainbow.

"MURDERERS," in blood red paint, screamed

signs that waved erratically, almost hitting one Marine as he descended the steps from the airplane. He was fresh out of Vietnam. His first step on American soil was greeted with a slurry of obscenities and spit in his face. I watched in disbelief. Living in a small town all my life, I had never seen anything like that.

"Jesus Christ," my dad muttered, and leaned forward with his elbows on his knees, watching the scene unfold in front of our eyes. He chugged down the last of his Lucky Lager and made his way to the kitchen. I turned the channel, but the same scene was playing out with a different news reporter.

I really hoped Karoline would find something else to do on this night. I'm not sure my dad would understand any reason for protesting soldiers who were serving their country, but he let my older siblings make their own decisions, now that they were eighteen and over, and considered adults.

My dad was a soft-spoken man, and even though he disagreed with the protesters, I knew he wouldn't say anything to Karoline if she chose to join in on the protest. She would learn by life experience, but he and my mom would still welcome her at every dinner table meal.

As I was drying the dishes, I could hear snippets of the adults' conversation in the living room, which centered on Jesse. It didn't sound like Mrs. Peters had heard any news of Jesse's whereabouts. Winnie and I looked at each other, trying not to alert Roo to our eavesdropping. She hadn't spilled the beans so far about seeing Jesse, but who knew when she would decide to blurt it out.

It was later that night as I lay asleep when the sounds of raised voices woke me up. Winnie and Roo were blinking their eyes and sitting up in their beds.

The clock in our room said 12:25 AM, and I knew something was wrong. My mom was an early to bed early to rise kind of person, so it was weird that she was awake. Dad, on the other hand, liked to stay up to watch the ten o'clock news, but usually dozed off during the sports report.

Right now, it sounded like everyone was awake and having a loud discussion in the kitchen. Winnie, Roo, and I scurried down the stairs in our bare feet, into the light of the kitchen. My mom on the phone and my dad talking to Duke, whose face was glistening with sweat as he bent over, hands on his knees trying to catch his breath.

"What's going on?" Winnie frowned, looking from Duke to my dad, and finally to my mom who had just hung up the phone.

"There is a situation at the Capitol," my dad said, "and we are trying to locate Karoline and Jack."

"What? What happened?" I ran up and hugged my mom, worried that they had been hurt.

"Duke and Jack went to the Capitol to see if people were protesting," my dad said, his brows furrowed, trying to recall the story. "Duke, tell me again what happened."

Duke took a deep breath and exhaled. He appeared as though he had just run a marathon, as he wiped the sweat off his forehead with his sleeve. "Well, Jack and I took the Buick down Sixth Avenue toward the

159

Capitol. We decided to park the car a few blocks away, so we didn't get blocked in," Duke talked as fast as an auctioneer.

"Slow down, son," my dad grasped Duke's shoulder.

Duke swallowed heavily and continued, "As we walked toward Montana Avenue, we were surprised to see such a massive crowd covering the lawn of the Capitol and even spilling into the street. You wouldn't have believed it," Duke shook his head, "some protesters were walking around with really obnoxious signs, like *U.S. SOLDIERS ARE MURDERERS* and another one had *BABY KILLERS* plastered all over it."

"Now, that's just not right," Duke was irritated. "Those soldiers are over there defending our country, and some of them sacrificed everything. Every... thing," he shook his head. His hands were on his hips, teeth biting his bottom lip. He studied the ceiling, trying to keep the gravitational pull of the tears inside his eyes from falling to the floor.

Finally, he looked at my dad, his voice was barely a whisper, and cracked as he continued, "How about Oly Andersen? Oly Andersen will never walk this earth again," his voice was bitter. "Charlie Andersen will never be the best man at his brother's wedding... Mr. and Mrs. Andersen will visit their son in a cemetery, and those bastards," he pointed out the door, "those low life, ungrateful bastards," he whispered, "will still have the freedom to wave their signs and spew their garbage."

We were all stunned at the anger in Duke's voice. This was out of his character; it took a lot to rile him.

Playing sports, school, and life in general always appeared to come so easily to Duke, only our family knew how much practice and effort it took for him to be at the top of his game. Watching his friends join the military over that past year had been weighing heavily on him, but he dealt with it in silence.

Roo ran over and hugged Duke's leg, "It's okay, Duke," she broke the silence, and he lifted her up.

"Sorry, Roo," Duke's voice softened. Her little arms were clasped so tightly around his neck, there would be no prying her away.

We all had forgotten that Roo had been listening to the entirety of Duke's retelling of the events, swear words and all. I know my mom didn't try to talk her into going back to bed because it would have been a battle, and she didn't have time for that.

My dad cleared his throat, "It's difficult to wrap your head around," he said quietly, "yes, it is," he nodded, confirming his statement. "I know Oly would not agree with their stance or the hateful words. In fact, I'm sure he would have had some terse words for those protesters if he were here." My dad paused, but a smile formed at the corners of his mouth, because we all knew Oly did not hold back when it came to speaking his mind. His teachers could give testament to that. Baseball umpires and football referees knew Oly would be nose to nose with them at the slightest hesitations and close calls. My dad went on, "But as hard as it is to hear, if Oly could do it all over again, I have no doubt, he would reenlist for their right to live in a land that will let them voice their opinions. No other soldiers in all of this world, have had to sacrifice so much for total strangers, in the name of liberty, justice, and freedom, than our American soldiers."

My mom wiped her nose with the tissue from her pocket. Her generation had felt the pains of World War II, less than thirty years earlier, and she would always remember classmates and friends who had left for the Pacific theater and never returned.

She pulled Duke in and hugged him so tight, probably wishing she could make things better, like she did when he was younger. She kissed his cheek, "I'm sorry son."

Duke began relaying the events and pried Roo loose, "most people there were booing and yelling back at the protesters," he paused and put his hands in his pockets, "Jack and I included..."

Duke continued, "Jack and I had just made our way to the statue of Thomas Meagher on the Capitol steps, when all of the sudden, we heard screams. One of the protesters, who happened to be a girl, was pushed to the ground by some guy in a football jersey. Another hippie-looking guy, probably her boyfriend, punched the football player in the face, and then they both really started going after each other." Duke paused, "That's when all hell broke loose."

"I climbed up on to the horse of the Thomas Meagher statue, so I could get a better view," he explained. "The second I got above the crowd, I heard someone calling my name, and knew it was Karoline. I scanned the crowd and saw Karoline waving at me, trying to get my attention. We locked eyes, but not a split second went by, and she got elbowed by a guy with a peace sign painted on his chest.

162

I yelled at Jack and pointed toward Karoline. He found her, but then," Duke paused again and rubbed his cheek with his hand, "Jack turned and pulled the guy up by his long hair. He lifted him up and chucked him into the crowd of protesters. You should have seen it! Holy shit, that guy flew like a rag doll!" Duke smiled in awe.

"The only thing was, the people that he landed on, weren't too happy," Duke's eyebrows raised, "and three guys started after Jack. I jumped off the statue and started running toward them, but by the time I made my way through the crowd, Jack had turned in to a combination of Bruce Lee and Steve McQueen and had Kung Fu'd and punched two of them.

I approached the third one and tackled him to the ground. That's when Karoline came and hit the guy with his, "*GIVE PEACE A CHANCE*," sign. Duke shook his head and laughed at that last bit.

My mom had her hand over her mouth in disbelief, half in awe and half in shock that her children were involved in such a scuffle.

"Well," Duke continued, "that's when we heard the sirens and every police car in town came screaming around the corner. The crowd started running, and we did, too. Somehow, I lost Jack and Karoline in the crowd. I headed across Montana Avenue toward Jack's car, thinking we would meet up there. I waited for a few minutes, but there were policemen coming down Sixth Avenue, so I ran down an alley and decided to just keep running home. Hopefully, Jack and Karoline are somewhere behind me."

Winnie and I followed my mom as she walked out the front door and stood on our porch looking up and down the street. We could hear sirens in the distance, and I wondered if Jack or Karoline was inside one of the vehicles. In a way, I was hoping they were safe inside a police car, and not being trampled or hurt in the crowd.

My dad, Roo, and Duke joined us on the front porch. "Dad," Duke was saying, "the protesters weren't even from Helena. There were three buses parked near the Capitol with out of state plates. A bunch of strangers came to our town to make a ruckus, and then leave in the night."

"That's not right," my mom sighed, "this is a peaceful town." She walked out to the sidewalk and looked up and down for signs of Karoline and Jack. "Where are they?" She crossed her arms and stared up the street, willing the car to turn the corner and head home.

Mrs. Peters yelled from across the street to my mom, "Is everything okay, dear? I've heard a lot of sirens this evening."

My mom didn't want to worry Mrs. Peters, "Oh, Mrs. Peters, there was a demonstration at the Capitol, but I think the police have a handle on it. We are just waiting for Jack and Karoline to come home. I'm sure everything is okay."

Then, as if on cue, I spotted the Buick speeding down the street. "Mom, there they are!" I ran to the curb as they parked and opened the passenger door to let Karoline out. Jack turned off the engine and jumped out of the car. As soon as he stood under the streetlight, I could see a shiner starting to form on his right eye. "Whoa, Jack, what happened to your eye?" I asked.

He lifted his hand to touch the outer part of his eye and winced. "It's Karoline's fault," he smiled.

Karoline shot him a smiling glance, "I suppose it was partly my fault," she smiled and looked sheepishly at mom and dad. "Jack and Duke saved me from some jerk at the demonstration. I'm glad they were there, not sure what I would have done otherwise."

"I'm pretty sure you could've held your own. The way you clobbered that guy with his own sign, I'm sure he has a few bruises to talk about," Jack laughed. "Maybe now he will take advice from his own sign and give peace a chance."

We all laughed as we made our way inside the house. Mrs. Peters shuffled back into her house, too. Just as I was closing our screen door, my heart skipped a beat, when I noticed someone sitting next to the tree at the triangle park. I blinked my eyes and peered into the darkness, trying to focus, and make out the shadowy form. It no longer looked like a person, but most likely the shadows from the trees, playing tricks on my eyes. At least that's what I told myself.

CHAPTER 20

The following day, I filled Jilly in on the events of the previous night. She knew most of what happened because Duke had called Jane, and of course Jilly listened to their whole conversation on the second phone line, that's how we usually got our best information. Jane said her parents had tuned in to their police scanner and fourteen people had been taken to the police station.

We were headed to the school. We agreed we should tell Jesse that he needed to go visit with his grandma. Mrs. Peters deserved the truth.

"Jilly, I don't think he's here… I don't think he's anywhere. We haven't seen him in a lot of days. He's vanished into thin air." We made our way through the broken window, trying to be quiet, so we didn't disturb any ghostly visitors, or frighten Jesse if he was sleeping.

"Man, you don't think something bad happened to him? You know, he didn't look good the last time we saw him," Jilly frowned.

I bit the inside of my lip, my mind, retraced the

conversations we'd had with Jesse. He wouldn't have gone to the hospital to ask for help, he seemed to be afraid to let anyone know he was here. What if he had walked somewhere and is too ill to come back to the school? Where else would he go? Maybe he was inside the building and too weak to get up.

Once we were all the way inside, we paused to let our eyes adjust to the darkness and began to cruise the perimeter of the classroom. As I made my way around the corner desk, my foot accidentally kicked something. Jilly and I both let out gasps of air and froze mid-step as we heard the object clatter down the aisle and clank against the leg of a desk.

Jilly's eyes were huge as her hand covered her mouth. Our eyeballs found each other's while our heads remained still as statues. I finally gave in, my eyes slowly lowering to observe what had rolled down the aisle.

I followed the trail on the dusty floor and stopped at a can of Campbell's soup, wedged next to a desk leg. It was the soup I had given to Jesse. Then I noticed the other food we had given to him, still beneath the desk near my feet. "Why didn't he eat the food we brought for him?" I asked Jilly.

"Huh?" Jilly squeaked, still standing frozen in time.

"Look," I pointed to the cans under the desk.

"What the..." Jilly relaxed and leaned over to examine them more closely.

"Why didn't he eat the food?" I repeated and bent down and picked up the chicken noodle soup and can of chili. The peanut butter and jelly sandwich looked slightly moldy inside the baggie.

"What the heck?" Jilly put her hands on her hips."

I put the soup down and clasped my hands together on the top of my head as though I was keeping it from floating into the atmosphere. "I have no idea," I said.

"Let's get out of here," Jilly said, "this place is giving me the chills, for real. Do you feel that?" It suddenly felt as cold as an ice box in the classroom.

Jilly and I skittered out of the building and walked in silence down Warren Street. I was about to ask Jilly how that room had turned so cold in the 90-degree heat, when she blurted out, "Oh, I almost forgot, Jane gave me two tickets to *The Aristocats!* She's babysitting tonight, so she can't go."

I halted to a standstill and looked at her as if she had gone mad. Two seconds ago, we were worried about weird vibes in the school and the possibility of being chased by some apparition, and now Jilly was wondering about a movie?

"I had a dog once," I smirked at her, restating the punch line of an old joke. One of our classmates had a knack for changing subjects right in the middle of a conversation. A while back, Davy had been upset as he discussed the fact that his grandma had been taken away in an ambulance the night before, and was mid-sentence when our classmate interrupted, "I had a dog once…" and proceeded to tell some random story about her dog being hurt. So, after that, whenever someone changed the subject, we retorted with, "I had a dog once…"

"Oops," Jilly shrugged, "I just didn't want to forget to tell you."

We had been waiting months for that movie to come to the Marlow Theater, but I didn't comment. My fingers could still feel the chill of that classroom.

"What's wrong? I thought you would be excited," Jilly put a hand on my shoulder, and we stopped walking.

"I dunno, I guess my head is full of Jesse," I shook my head trying to change gears. "Sorry, I do want to go to that movie. I'm pretty sure my mom will let me; she knows I have been wanting to see it." My mouth started watering thinking about the giant dill pickles they sold at the concession stand.

CHAPTER 21

Going to the Marlow Theater was a big deal. There had been talk around town that the Marlow was on the urban renewal chopping block, and its days were numbered. Jilly and I were devastated when we heard the rumors.

The Marlow Theater was a regal building, complete with gargoyles, grand high arches, bright carpeting and the softest of seats that tired mothers were known to doze in, as they sat with their children during Saturday afternoon matinees.

Back in the day, road shows and vaudeville acts came from across the country to perform on its stage, draped in velvet curtains and surrounded by ornate details reminiscent of the Renaissance. The ceiling was a work of art, and the floors in the grand lobby and mezzanine looked like they belonged in a palace.

The town went wild when two of Helena's own, visited the Marlow Theater. Myrna Loy, and later, Gary Cooper, for his premiere of *The Naked Edge*. John F. Kennedy made an appearance at the Marlow during the

1960 Montana Democratic Convention, accompanied by his brother Ted Kennedy. So, you can imagine the upheaval when the people of our town heard this grand building was going to be demolished.

The movie was packed with kids, and a few adults scattered in between, during the seven o'clock show. Giant dill pickles in hand, we staked our claim in the balcony, typically occupied by the junior high crowd.

Tommy Benson and Sean Wilson sat next to us during the movie. That would remain top-secret information, a tidbit I would not be sharing with my mom, unless she asked me very specific questions. Girls in our family were not allowed to date until sixteen years of age.

When the movie was over, we parted ways with Tommy and Sean and headed down Warren Street. By the time we reached our neighborhood, the streetlights had not yet turned on.

Jilly and I sat down on my front porch steps to finish off the last of my Milk Duds. We were making plans to meet the next morning, for our final baton practice before the Kiddie's Parade the following day, when an old station wagon pulled alongside the curb and sputtered to a stop.

The engine made a moaning sound as the driver turned the key to restart the car. All the windows were rolled down and someone in the back seat told the driver to try it again.

"It's on empty, Janis," the driver said impatiently. He laid his head on the seat back behind him and rubbed his face like I had seen my dad do when he was tired, after a long car ride. Then, as though he realized the

171

predicament he was in, he slammed his hands back down on the steering wheel showing his frustration.

"What now?" Janis sounded worried from that back seat.

"I don't know," the driver said, still impatient.

"What?" she asked, "what did you say?" she sounded a little more frantic.

"I said, I don't know!" he yelled, in a mad sing song voice.

The box of Milk Duds was empty, so I popped my last piece of bubblegum into my mouth, as we continued to watch the drama being played out in front of my house, elbows on knees, chins cradled in our hands. None of the six people in the car were aware of Jilly and me sitting there.

The streetlights popped on, but Jilly hesitated in leaving because she didn't want to miss this soap opera happening before us. The only excitement we ever had on this street was when Mr. Magoo decided to take a drive, now we had a real live *Peyton Place* showing in front of my house. Jilly opted to take any consequence her parents would dish out for being late in getting home. This drama was too good to pass up.

We suddenly heard her mom's voice in the distance, calling from their back porch, "Jil-ly, time to come home!" Jilly didn't flinch, hoping her mom would just go back inside knowing her daughter had heard her calling. But then once more a little louder, "JIL-LY!" and I heard Jilly groan as she rolled her eyes. Jilly thought better of disregarding her curfew and high-tailed it home. That was when one of the kids in the back seat noticed us.

Muffled voices started a discussion in the car and then the driver called out, "Hey, kid!" He looked at me. I stood there, not knowing if I should answer because of the whole stranger danger thing. "Hey, kid!" he said again, and they all had turned in my direction. "Don't worry, we aren't mass murderers or anything," everyone in the car laughed.

He had eerily read my mind. Charles Manson's murder sprees in California had been a hot topic in the news that year. Every time I saw Manson's face on the news, it gave me the heebie-jeebies. He was a picture of pure evil, and his followers seemed to be the same age as these kids in this car. I stepped onto my lawn, a safe sidewalk away from their car.

"Hey kid, is your mom home?" the driver asked. He didn't really look like a mass murderer, but I would have told him my mom was home, even if she wasn't, I wasn't going to take any chances. I for sure wasn't going to tell him my dad was at his barbershop quartet practice right then, either.

"Um, yeah," I answered, bending over to look deeper into the car. At first glance, the sea of long hair made me think it was all girls in the car. But a closer look at the beards and mustaches, I realized there were four boys and two girls, who all appeared to be in their early twenties.

"We need some help. Do you think you could get your mom?" he asked.

"Just a minute," I said to the driver and I ran inside and found my mom in the kitchen on the phone.

"Mom! Mom! Can you come outside?" I was whispering yelling, since she was on the phone.

Her brows furrowed as she mouthed the word "No," and waved me away, pointing to the phone as though I didn't see her holding it next to her ear.

"Mom, please come out," I pointed to the front door, "there is a strange car outside. I think they are in trouble!" She finally noticed my urgency and told whoever she was talking to that she would call them back.

"What in the world is going on, Betts?" my mom asked.

"Some kids ran out of gas in front of our house, and I think they are stuck, and don't know what to do!" I pointed out front again. "They asked me to get you."

My mom walked to the living room and looked out the front window, her hand on her cheek, trying to decide if she should go out there or not.

"I think they are in trouble, I said. They have California license plates, too."

My mom's eyes squinted, trying to make out the shapes in the car. "You don't think they are part of Charles Manson's followers, do you?" I asked, parting the sheer curtains covering our large front room window to get a better look. Her eyes grew wide, and she looked sideways at me, trying to process what I had just said, her fingers tapped her upper lip as she thought.

After some hesitation, she surmised, "I wonder if they were with the protesters from last night. They probably came to town for the demonstration," and she

174

headed out the front door. I wasn't sure if she was going to help them or scold them.

After talking with my mom, it turns out they were unaware of the demonstration. They were musicians and had hit the road from California hoping to play some gigs along the way to Glacier Park. They were supposed to stay with a friend in Helena, but there was a mix-up, and that plan had changed. To make matters worse, they were out of money.

Having six kids in our family, my parents didn't really have a lot of extra money laying around the house, especially since we had Karoline's wedding coming up later that summer. We could probably spare ten or twenty dollars, but those kids were going to need more money than that to make it back to California. My mom would never leave them stranded, though. They were so close to Jack, Duke, and Karoline's ages, she hoped strangers would do the same for them if they ever needed help.

My mom called Father Dolan at the Cathedral to see if the church could help in some way. She must have decided they truly weren't mass murderers, because she invited them into our house while we waited for Father Dolan to arrive and heated up the leftovers from dinner. They obviously hadn't eaten in a while because every dish was emptied before Father Dolan rang our doorbell.

Roo had followed all of this without saying a word. She was mesmerized watching these strangers wolf down last night's dinner. Winnie came in from being at the Senators' baseball game right then, too. Her eyeballs moved from face to face sitting around our kitchen table, not recognizing a single one.

My mom opened her mouth to explain, but Roo beat her to it. "Hi Winnie! They ran out of gas," she shrugged her shoulders. "Father Dolan is coming to fill 'er up," she said cheerily, giving a thumb's up. "Don't worry," she put her hand next to her mouth and whispered, "they aren't mass murderers, they're just really, really hungry!" Roo's eyes opened wide as she nodded her head. Her voice grew deeper, "I mean REALLY HUNGRY!" and she emphasized by using her arms to pantomime a huge stomach. Everybody laughed.

"Uh," Winnie looked like a deer in the headlights, "hello," she said slowly, still looking like she was in the Twilight Zone or something.

"They had a little car trouble in front of the house, and we thought they might be hungry," my mom smiled at Winnie. "Father Dolan is coming here to see if we can help them to get on their way. They didn't realize it would be quite so expensive to travel by car, even with six of them splitting the tab. Gas prices these days..." and she shook her head without finishing the sentence.

"I was happy to leave LA for a while, that place gets a little intense at times," the girl named, Linda, revealed. "I can definitely see why Montana is called the Big Sky State, it is absolutely breathtaking, and the air smells so fresh, like pine or something."

Her thoughts were interrupted by the rat-a-tat of rapid machine gun fire blaring from the ten o'clock news on the living room TV. Of course, the news reporter was featuring a story from Vietnam, the news was always about Vietnam. We could barely make out his words as he was yelling over the whirring of helicopter blades circling above his head.

176

"Betts, will you turn that off, please?" my mom asked. "We don't need to listen to that tonight."

Glen, the driver of the car nodded, "Thank you, we appreciate that," and he smiled at my mom. "We just went to the funeral of a good friend of ours a few days ago. Twenty-three years old," he took a drink of water. "He's the reason we're here. After the funeral, Henley here," and he pointed to his buddy, "said he needed to get out of there. I thought he meant get out of the funeral home, but he meant get out of the state. That's when we just jumped in the car and took off driving, without any real plans, just hoping to play some gigs along the way. Didn't really stop until we landed in front of your house."

"I'm so sorry to hear that," my mom said quietly. "Our neighbor is still waiting to hear word of her grandson. He has been listed as missing in action. It's been difficult for her not knowing."

He nodded and so did everyone else at the table. "I'm sorry to hear that. Do they have any idea of his location before he went missing?" Glen asked.

"Possibly at the siege of Khe Sanh," my mom answered.

He shook his head, "Yeah, there was some heavy fire power there. It sounded like it was pretty rough." He paused, and the soft clanking of forks continued. He finally looked up at my mom, "I hope your friend's grandson makes it home," and he nodded his head revealing a sad smile, his eyes far away. I had a feeling he meant he had hoped Jesse came home whether it was in a body bag or not.

Missing in action was a lifelong sorrow for

families who would never have answers about their missing sons or daughters. They would live forever wondering where their child rested each night when the sun went down.

It was after ten-thirty when Father Dolan arrived. Most gas stations in town would have been closed by then, so he brought his lawn mower gas can to give them enough fuel to make it to the gas station in the morning. He discussed the situation with all of us and said he would be able to help them out. "I will have to file a request for funds from Catholic Services in the morning, it shouldn't take too long, in the meantime, we will have to find a place for you to spend the night."

My mom, of course, offered our back yard. She wouldn't think of letting them sleep in their car or at the homeless shelter downtown. Having grown up in the wheat fields of central Montana during the depression, she was the second oldest of seven children that lived with their parents in a small farmhouse. Her father worked for the railroad and would often bring home complete strangers who had been riding the rails, to share a warm, home cooked meal. My grandparents had next to nothing, but they always figured out a way to turn nothing into something.

My mom shared that same tenderness, especially for the elderly and children. Many times, we were with her when she picked up our gray-haired neighbors to give them rides to church or the store or checked in on them to make sure they were okay. We often had friends over for dinner when times were tight at their own houses.

That night, when my dad opened the back-yard gate to six complete strangers sleeping on his lawn, he wouldn't question it. He would probably say something like, "What the hell...?" But then, would figure my mom would hàve a good explanation.

Later that night, as we lay in bed, I could hear the soft strumming of a guitar. Roo was already asleep, but Winnie and I ran to look out Karoline's open bedroom window in the back of the house. They sat on the sleeping bags singing something about a hotel in California. It was a little eerie, but I liked it. We wanted to stay and listen to more, but it was late, and my mom yelled up the stairs for us to get to bed.

Back in our beds, Winnie whispered to me, "Did you see Jesse today?"

"No, no we didn't. And do you want to know what is so weird?" I asked, and didn't wait for an answer, "when Jilly and I went inside the classroom, we didn't see one trace of Jesse." I lifted on to my elbow, "The soup, peanut butter and jelly sandwich, carton of water, they were all still there," I paused, "untouched!" I whispered a little louder. "He didn't eat anything we brought for him! Kind of weird, don't you think?"

"Yeah, that's kind of strange. The way you described him, he sounded like he was near death and needed food before he keeled over," Winnie remarked.

We both laid there, replaying the strange turn of events that had happened that day, watching shadows of tree branches dancing on our ceiling, until our heavy eyelids finally drooped and closed.

CHAPTER 22

I wanted to hang around and talk to our backyard guests when they woke up, but I had parade rehearsal and couldn't miss it. My mom had stayed home from work to make breakfast for them and meet Father Dolan at St. Helena's. By the time I returned home, they were gone, but my mom said they had left something for me.

"Glen, you know, the driver?" she reminded me, "said they didn't have much, but they wanted you to have this," and she handed me a heavy Buttery's grocery bag. There was a note written on the outside of the bag that had my name on it:

Betts,

Thank you for being brave and taking
a chance on us not being mass murderers.

Take it easy,
Glen F.

I looked inside and saw several record albums and pulled one out. "Oh, my gosh, The Beatles – *Abbey Road,*" I said in awe as I searched the back of the album for the song list. I grabbed another one, "*Sgt. Pepper's Lonely-Hearts Club Band!*" I was getting more and more excited. Three more albums were inside, The Beatles-*Hard Day's Night,* The Beach Boys-*Pet Sounds,* and Crosby, Stills and Nash. "I can't believe they left all of this for me!"

This was a jackpot of albums sitting in a brown paper bag on my kitchen table, and they were mine. I had only one album in my collection, and that was *The Archie's Greatest Hits.* Of course, I cherished and deemed to it be a musical masterpiece. Albums were expensive, so if we wanted to have other music on hand, we couldn't go out and buy expensive albums, we would call KCAP and request the song from the DJ. We would wait hours sitting next to the radio, with our finger hovering over the red record button on our cassette player, hoping to get a recording of a favorite song. So, having such iconic music in my hands, on real vinyl LP's, was beyond satisfying.

The Beatles had broken up, which meant their albums were in high demand. For those kids in the beat-up station wagon to have given up such a treasure, they must have been grateful for my help. Those albums would follow me through life, even when record players had become obsolete, reminding me that karma was real.

I grabbed The Beach Boys *Pet Sounds* album and placed it on our turntable in the basement. Brian Wilson's falsetto broke the silence, and *Wouldn't It Be Nice,* filled the cool basement, crooning about young lovers expressing the need to have the freedom to live together. As I sat back in my mom's old green armchair, I was lost in the music, singing along and memorizing every detail on the record jacket. By the time the needle reached *God Only Knows,* I was completely enveloped, experiencing a deep yearning to be the first female member of The Beach Boys.

However, the previous two late nights had taken a toll on me, and I was jolted awake two hours later by my mom's voice asking me to set the table for dinner. I took care to lift the album off the record player and place it back into the album cover and ran upstairs.

My stomach grumbled at the smell of pork chops baking in the oven and potatoes boiling on the stove. "Hello, sleepyhead," my mom laughed. "You have been sleeping for two hours! I think you were trying to catch up on sleep from that past two late night shenanigans. What a week this has been," she smiled and shook her head.

I grinned back at my mom and grabbed the plates to set the table. It had been a wild week, a wild summer, really, one I would remember for a long time, and I hadn't even performed in the parade yet. The parade was tomorrow and trying to contain my excitement was going to be difficult. Jilly and I had practiced for hours and hours and we knew that routine frontwards and backwards. The parade was going to be the highlight of our summer.

I could hardly sleep that night, and at the first crack of sunlight through my window shade, I popped out of bed. My mom and dad and the older three kids bustled about the house getting ready for work. I knew taking time off from work for the parade was an impossibility for them, and my parents especially felt bad that they couldn't be there. Winnie was directed to take Polaroid pictures of the event so it was documented in our family history, and Roo would be by her side.

The Kiddies' Parade began at eleven o'clock and Jilly and I were at Women's Park downtown an hour before that, with batons in hand, dressed in our white shirts, blue cut off shorts, moccasins, and red bandannas tied around our neck. Evidence of the lack of budget, plus her own lame interpretation of the Blackfeet nation that had lived at the base of Mt. Helena during the gold rush years, our young instructor gave us headbands with a couple feathers attached, and painted stripes on our faces.

The park buzzed with miniature versions of cowboys and miners, clowns and baton twirlers. Dogs were barking at cats in cages and the whinny of nervous horses scared babies dressed as dolls in baby carriages. The junior high band tuned their instruments to the sound of a howling beagle dressed as a ballerina. How the parade organizers were going to turn the chaotic scene into a parade, was anyone's guess.

Someone blew a whistle, and we turned to see a short stout woman who appeared to be dressed as a boy scout, waving a clip board in the air. She wore khaki pants with a matching shirt, complimented with a red bandanna around her neck held together by a gold ring. Her black curly hair could barely be tamed by the round stiff-brimmed hat she wore. Her pants were stuffed into tall boots that I had seen jockeys wear during horse races. The crowd had trouble finding the source of the whistle, since the woman was only as tall as the kids around her, until she finally stood on a huge boulder and whistled again.

She somehow managed to arrange everyone into parade order, and we started walking toward Last Chance Gulch. Jilly and I looked at each other and grinned with excitement. The band fired up and the Boy Scouts presenting the colors led the way.

Our twirling group started marching and performing our routine to *Hawaii Five-o,* as we made our way down Last Chance Gulch. The street was lined with storekeepers, moms and dads, grandmas and grandpas, and brothers and sisters, all watching the line of kids coming down the street. I was surprised to see Mrs. Peters had ventured out of the neighborhood, and stood on the corner clapping and yelling, "Bravo, Betts! Bravo for you!"

Have you ever had one of those times in your life when something totally unexpected happens that causes you to feel so proud you think you will burst with joy? This was one of those moments. Here we were, at the pinnacle of the summer, finally marching in the Kiddie's Parade. There was something so sweet, so perfectly wonderful about seeing Mrs. Peters on that corner yell my name that my eyes began to sting, and a stupidly wide grin formed like I had just won an Olympic gold medal.

Jilly did a double take as she noticed my watering eyes. "Are you okay?" she mouthed the words.

"Best day ever," I beamed.

I searched for Winnie and Roo in the crowd. Winnie told me they would be standing a couple blocks away, in front of The Parrot, a local confectionery known for their homemade chocolates and old-fashioned soda fountain. We were meeting there after the parade to have a Mexican Lime and a bowl of chili, topped off with a piece of homemade candy for dessert, Mom's treat.

Walking into the Parrot was like taking a step back in time, virtually unchanged since 1938. Voices of Frank Sinatra, The Andrews Sisters, and Elvis filled the air from the old jukebox nestled amid the green wooden booths, that claimed the initials of young couples in love and teenagers who just wanted to be remembered. The lunch counter, complete with a soda fountain, was bordered by silver swiveling red vinyl cushioned stools, that high school sweethearts perched on as far back as the Roosevelt administration. It was one of our favorite places in all of Helena.

But the Parrot was not meant to be that day. We had just marched past JC Penney, a store who claimed the only escalator in town, when I saw Winnie, not watching the parade, but looking frantically among the crowd of people on the sidelines. As we marched by, I stopped twirling, distracted by her demeanor. I scanned the area for Roo, but she was nowhere to be seen. Winnie looked up and spotted me within the group of twirlers. She yelled out, "I can't find Roo! I've lost Roo!" She looked genuinely upset and I finally stopped marching, causing the girl behind me to hit me in the head with her baton.

Jilly looked confused and watched me run to the sidelines. "Keep going, I'll be right back," I yelled to her.

"Winnie, what happened?" I grabbed her arm.

She was visibly upset. "Skip followed us," she said, her arms up in the air, "and we yelled at him to go home, but of course, he didn't, that little..." she paused, not wanting to say a bad word. "We could see you coming, and I didn't want to miss you, so I just ignored him, hoping he would hang around near us, or go home. Then, one of the dogs on the buffalo jump float leaped from the float, and started running up Lawrence toward the Cathedral, with Skip on his tail. I told Roo we would get him after you went by, but I think she took off after him when I wasn't looking."

Winnie and I started running up Lawrence Street, which is one of the steepest streets in Helena, so we were breathing heavily by the time we were in front of the Cathedral. The dogs and Roo were nowhere in sight. "Roo!" I yelled and put my hands on my knees to catch my breath. I yelled again, and Winnie joined in. We circled around the Cathedral, but there was no trace of the dogs or Roo.

"ROO!" Winnie shrieked. She was getting frantic. "Betts, where is she?" Her voice was shaking.

"We'll find her. Don't get upset. We will find her," I repeated, trying to reassure my own self. "Roo!" I started yelling again.

We ran down Warren Street toward our house, thinking Skip may have headed home with Roo on his heels. We ran inside and circled around to the back yard, but no sign of them. Back toward the Cathedral we went, yelling as we ran. As we passed the Cathedral, Father Dolan was crossing the parking lot, cane in hand, and hollered to us, "Is everything okay?"

"Father Dolan," I panted, "we can't find Roo. She was watching the parade with Winnie, but suddenly disappeared. We think she is following our dog, Skip," I put my hands on my head trying to breathe, as my eyes scanned the area. "Have you seen Roo or Skip?"

"I'm sure she's not far. Maybe she is still downtown on the parade route. Why don't you go back down and double check the parade route and I will look around here? As we ran off, he yelled, "Ladies, have faith. We will find her," and he began limping quickly around the parking lot, checking in the parked cars.

We scanned the parade route, asking anyone we saw if they had seen a little girl with Roo's description or a dog with Skip's description, but no one had noticed them. Almost an hour had passed, but it seemed more like five hours. We had run the full length of Last Chance Gulch, checking inside stores and along alleyways. We heard a dog barking near Yat Son's Noodle Parlor and ran to investigate, but it was not Skip.

"Oh my god, Winnie, where is she?" I cried; we had stopped to catch our breath. "We need to find her," I started sobbing.

Winnie grabbed me and hugged me so tight, I lost my breath. I know, I know," her voice cracked, "we need to keep going, Betts, we can't waste time. Let's run up to the Fire Tower hill, and maybe we can get a better view from up there." She pulled the neckline of her t-shirt up over her face to wipe her eyes and nose and grabbed my hand, "C'mon, let's find Roo," she said, sounding determined.

We ran straight up Broadway, and then uphill once more to the highest point near the old Fire Tower. My legs were on fire as I pushed to get to the top, but I didn't care. I wasn't going to stop until I found my little sister. The sunny day didn't make things easier, with another record-breaking temperature.

Our shirts were plastered to our backs as we reached the top of the hill, and I figured my face was probably the same shade of red as Winnie's. I was dying for a cold drink of water to quench my sandpaper throat or even pour on top of my head. I licked my dry lips and shaded my eyes with my hand, squinting, trying to focus on the people milling about below us.

This was going to be impossible, I thought to myself. There were too many people, and buildings, and trees lining the streets blocked our complete view. "This isn't going to work," I said, "we are wasting time."

"Yeah, you're right," Winnie kept looking and then put her hand down. "We need to go home," she paused and took a deep breath, "we need to call Mom."

"She is going to be so upset," my voice broke. The sudden mention of Mom opened the flood gates, and tears washed down my cheeks, as I pictured my mom's face draining of its blood and turning stark white when we told her that her baby girl is missing.

"Yeah, but we can't do this alone," Winnie bit her lip, "let's go," she gave me a tight squeeze. We took off back down Fire Tower Hill, down Warren Street past the Cathedral, and the four blocks to our house. I cried as I ran, which made it hard to breathe and keep up the pace. "Betts, you need to stop crying, we are going to find her," Winnie reassured me.

Mrs. Peters was at the top of the block, probably just getting home from watching the parade. Winnie spotted her first, "Mrs. Peters," she ran across the street, "Mrs. Peters, did you happen to see Roo?"

"No, I haven't seen her, was she in the parade, too?" she asked.

"No, she and I were watching the parade, but I lost her in the crowd, and now we can't find her," Winnie swallowed.

"I'm going to look in the house," I interrupted, and ran across the street and up our front steps.

"Oh dear," Mrs. Peters put her hand on her cheek, "she sure is a slippery little thing. I'm sure she will show up. I wonder if she went to my house? Maybe she is in my backyard, let me go check to see if she is there."

Winnie met me in an empty house. No sign of Roo or Skip anywhere. While she got on the phone and dialed the hospital where my mom worked, I hastily guzzled two glasses of water.

It seemed to take forever for the receptionist to locate her, and my nervous energy took me outside to look up and down the block.

Mrs. Peters yelled from across the street, "I'm sorry, dear, she is not here!" She must have noticed my shoulders slump at her words, and stood looking at me for a minute, hand over her mouth. She called to me again, "Honey, come over here," motioning for me to join her on her front sidewalk. She put her arm around me in a hug and then pulled me close to look eye to eye. "Honey, you must believe," and to make her point clearer, "you must believe!" she whispered firmly and shook one finger in front of my face.

As I looked into her weary gray eyes, grief was their keeper. Every wrinkled crease beneath them, represented each loss in her life. I nodded my head, ever so slightly, but understood the anguish this little white-haired woman was experiencing, because another person was missing from her life. Hope was all she had left.

Winnie popped out of the front door and yelled, "Betts, Mom is on her way," and started running toward the park to meet her. I thanked Mrs. Peters and squeezed her hand and ran to catch up with Winnie. My mom met us in the middle of the park.

"Mom, I'm sorry!" Winnie broke down as we reached her, "I'm so sorry, she just disappeared," and the dam of tears burst, all the while hugging Mom and me as though she would never let go.

My mom pulled away from the hug and pulled her face close to Winnie's. Holding both of Winnie's cheeks, "Listen to me, we all know Roo, and we know how she wanders off, it could have happened to any of us. Do you hear me? It could have happened to *any* of us." She used the palms of her hands to wipe Winnie's cheeks. "What we need to do now is focus on finding her."

Winnie was the most responsible kid in our family. We all knew she would never forgive herself if anything happened to Roo, and even when we found Roo, she would have a hard time letting go of the guilt. I grabbed Winnie's hand and ran across the street toward our house.

My dad pulled up in the back of our house as a squad car pulled up in front. Having a policeman visit our house seemed surreal. I had never spoken face to face with any law enforcement officers in my life and seeing him sitting at our kitchen table was like being on an episode of Dragnet.

I had truly believed Roo would wander home any minute without a care in the world, just like she had done all the other times she had gone missing, so involving the police made it seem too real.

Winnie and I shared the story again, as the policeman took notes on a small notepad and asked, what seemed like a hundred questions. We were antsy to get back outside and continue the search and grew frustrated as each minute ticked by.

He asked for pictures of Roo and made a call to the police station, requesting back up. By then, a few neighbors had gathered in front of our house, including Jilly and her sisters, Father Dolan, and even Mr. Magoo. Duke, Karoline, and Jack had all gotten word, and pulled up as the officer was giving directions and dividing people up to search for Roo. Tommy and Shane sped up on their bikes. Even Alvin and three of his friends had somehow heard Roo was missing and ran up to our house.

The most surprising offers to help search for Roo were of all people, Harvey Dill and Rooster. "Tommy told me about your sister, and we came to help look for her," Harvey glanced up from his feet and back down, shoving his hands in his pockets.

I could only nod. I felt like screaming. I wanted to tell everyone that Roo does this all the time, and she is probably just hiding. Having this crowd in front of our house meant that Roo was in real danger. It was real. This is something that one would only see on the news or movie of the week. I didn't even want to venture to think about the reasons children go missing, I was not going to let my mind go there.

The group split up to search the area between our house and downtown. My mom stayed home in case Roo, or Skip, found their way home, or someone called with information. She wanted Winnie and me to stay home, too, because she was worried something would happen to us, but we begged and pleaded for her to let us help in the search, and she eventually gave in.

To ease my mom's mind, Karoline stayed near

Winnie and me. We decided to go through the alleys on Warren Street, and head toward the Cathedral and beyond, to Central School. Our pace was slower than before, so we could make sure to check in between garages and fences and behind garbage cans, all the places a little girl could hide.

As we searched, I felt as though I was in an underwater dream, sinking downward, watching the sunlight fade from the surface. Garbled voices echoed Roo's name from all directions, voices that sounded like the slow speed on the record player. My mind was trying to register everything but couldn't make sense of anything. My legs just kept going through the motions, and my mouth kept yelling for Roo. Winnie and I had run what seemed like a marathon today, and we were still moving. But, as we ran along the sidewalk on the south side of the Cathedral, fatigue set in, and I tripped and fell face first, skidding down the sidewalk to a stop.

"Betts!" Winnie heard the slap of my palms hitting the cement behind her.

"Are you okay?" Karoline bent down to check on me. I didn't say anything at first, because I really didn't know if I was okay.

"Yeah," I rolled onto my back and covered my face with one arm.

"Oh, man, your arms and hands are scraped up," Karoline remarked.

"I'm fine," my monotone voice was muffled through my arm. Karoline and Winnie both sat down next to me, giving me time to breathe.

"Do you want to go home, Betts?" Winnie asked. "We should clean your scrapes."

"No! I said I'm fine," I snipped back at her, "just give me a second." We sat there in silence until I felt an anger inside me begin to surface. "Why does Roo always do this!" I yelled. "Why can't she just follow directions and quit making us go on wild goose chases every day of the week! Where in the hell is she?" I screamed, causing a poodle across the street to bark. "Where are you, Roo?" I shrieked, and the dog upped its high-pitched yapping.

As if on cue, the three of us turned toward the dog and yelled, "SHUT UP!" at exactly the same time, which broke the tension and made us smile.

I wiped my leaking nose with the back of my arm, and looked at my scratches, all the while wondering how this was going to play out. I turned to look behind me at the church and wondered where God was today.

"We should go inside and light a candle for Roo in Mary's Chapel," Winnie suggested when she saw me looking at the church.

"We should hurry, though," Karoline said. We stood up and hustled toward the huge wooden doors. Our tennis shoes squeaked on the polished floor as we walked ahead to the chapel area on the opposite side of the church. We genuflected as we passed the altar and I silently hoped God heard us come in.

At Mary's Chapel, we took long wooden matches and lit candles sitting on the altar, then knelt to say a quick prayer. I began to recite, "Hail Mary, full of grace, hallowed be-"

"GO!" a voice interrupted my prayer, and I opened my eyes. I looked behind me, but no one was there, so I resumed my prayer.

"GO!" the tone was more insistent. There was no denying I heard a voice. I stood and ran down the steps of the chapel and looked toward the pews, but still no one. Karoline and Lynn blessed themselves and caught up to me.

"Who was that?" I blurted, still scanning the pews.

"Who?" Karoline started to scan the pews because I was scanning the pews.

"Someone said to go," I turned around behind me to check the confessionals.

"What? I didn't hear anything," Winnie looked confused.

"Me either," shrugged Karoline, "what do you think they said?"

"He said..." and I realized they probably thought I was going bonkers, my voice trailed off.

"What the heck? You didn't hear anything? Nothing?" I looked at both of them. I dug for a wad of bubblegum in my jean shorts' pocket, and popped it in my mouth, trying to decide if I had heard a voice or not. "Sounded like Jesse," I must have said aloud.

"Jesse?" Karoline asked.

"It's a long story. Can I tell you later?" I asked.

Karoline looked at Winnie for an answer, but

Winnie just shrugged.

I chewed on the gum trying to soften it up. I didn't care that I was inside the church where gum was a no-no, gum made me think better. Suddenly I decided, "Let's go." Whether someone told me, or I imagined it, let's go," and we took off.

The second we pushed the church doors open, the smell of smoke caught our attention. "Do you smell smoke?" Karoline asked.

"Yeah, something is definitely on fire," Winnie sniffed, while scanning the area.

We all froze, and I could tell that my sisters had the same exact thought that had just exploded into my head. We turned to look at smoke coming out of the old high school across the street and sprinted for it. I don't know how, but we knew Roo had to be in there.

"God, Roo is in there!" I cried, and I wasn't sure if I was sharing that information with God, or my sisters. We barreled over the stone wall toward the back, where we had previously crawled through the broken window. Thick smoke was coming out of the second story and I didn't care if I got hurt or not, but I was going in that building.

"Betts! What are you doing?" Karoline yelled and was pulling on my arm. Suddenly, we heard a dog's faint bark from inside.

"Ssh, listen! I held up my hand, and we heard another series of barks.

Winnie yelled, "Skip? Skip? Come here boy!" We waited, but he didn't come out. He barked again, and again, and continued to bark.

By that point, all three of us were inside the window of the old school, yelling for Skip and Roo. I looked around the room for Jesse. The food we had given him was strewn about, so someone or something had been in here.

We followed the sound of Skip's bark and entered the hallway. The smoke was a thicker there than in the classroom, which made the hallway a hazy and eerie tunnel. I pulled the collar of my shirt up over my nose and mouth, trying to filter out some of the smoke. A small sliver of the evening sun seeped through the windows near the grand entrance, illuminating the billowing smoke.

We followed the barking. "He's upstairs," Winnie pointed and then coughed, trying to expel the inhaled smoke, "we need to hurry!" We all covered our mouths and stayed low to the stairs. As we got to the landing, a can of soup rolled across when my foot hit it. The now frantic barks were interspersed with whining, and I knew we were getting closer.

We crawled up the last five steps to the second floor and I began coughing and gagging. Karoline pulled at my arm and tapped Winnie and pointed for us to go back down. We had to; we couldn't breathe. As we hit the bottom stair, I could hear sirens in the distance and hoped this building was their mission.

Karoline shouted over the roar of the fire and Skip's panic attack, "You two stay here, I'm going back up!"

"I'm coming!" Winnie shouted back.

"No! It's too dangerous, just let me go!"

Suddenly, as Karoline turned to head up the stairs, Skip came bounding down them past Karoline and jumped on me, whining and licking my face.

"Oh my god! Where's Roo?" I cried as I looked back up the stairs, and trying to comfort a distressed, Skip. I couldn't take it, and bolted up the steps two at a time, not caring about the smoke or fire.

"Betts! Betts!" Winnie and Karoline screamed for me to return.

"Betts!" Winnie screamed and ran after me. "Go get help!" she screeched to Karoline and ran toward the second floor.

At the top of the stairs, a bright glow illuminated a classroom on the far end of the hallway opposite the fire. The light didn't flicker like a fire, but my instincts told me to head in that direction. As soon as we reached the doorway, the room suddenly went dark.

"Holy shit, I can't see!" I yelled at the sudden inky darkness.

We started yelling for Roo, and even though she didn't answer, I couldn't let go of the feeling that she was in this room. We were coughing and hacking. Slobber was coming out of our noses and mouths and we pulled the collars of our shirts up over our mouths to try to get some sort of respite from the smoke.

Finally, I tripped across a fallen bookshelf and miraculously stumbled upon Roo, whose legs were trapped under the bookcase. "Winnie!" I croaked, "Win…" my throat felt like sandpaper and it was impossible to get the words out. She saw my hand waving frantically and crawled over to find Roo lying motionless under the bookcase.

The bookcase was huge and made of a heavy wood; it was going to be impossible to move. Winnie and I tried to lift it, but it didn't budge. Winnie's voice Was raspy, "Betts, we need to hurry!"

I looked at the immense bookcase and rubbed my sweating hands on my back pockets. The situation was dire, and we had no time to wait for help. Roo looked like a rag doll and I knew it was up to Winnie and me to free her trapped legs. I motioned for Winnie to get ready to grab Roo's legs and I bent down and took hold of the wooden bookcase. I have no idea how I did it, but I gave it everything I had and lifted the bookcase just high enough for Winnie to pull Roo out from under it.

I grabbed Roo's shoulders as Winnie took hold of her feet. We carried her through the smoky corridor and down the steps to the first landing. We had to stop. The smoke was making it extremely difficult to exert so much energy carrying Roo and a coughing spasm made me throw up. I wasn't sure how we were going to make it out of the building, we still had to go down another flight of stairs.

"God, please help us out of here," I whispered, and wiped my eyes with my sleeve.

Winnie was stroking Roo's hair, "You're going to be okay… you're going to be okay. Roo, be strong, please, just be strong."

Suddenly, a form appeared at the top of the stairs. The

lighting from the windows and the smoky haze made it hard to see clearly. My heart was beating out of my chest, and I briefly thought about the ghost of the dead miner. Winnie and I could only sit there, unable to move.

As I watched him take one step after another, I thought my eyes were playing tricks on me, when I realized the form was wearing a helmet and boots, and the fatigues of a soldier. The straps of his helmet were hitting his cheeks with each step. Like a scene from a war movie, through the smoke and the flashing lights from the fire trucks pulling up outside, he reached down and lifted Roo's small lifeless body from Winnie's arms.

Winnie let go of Roo so easily, momentarily stunned. He descended the stairs as we sat dazed, thinking we were in a dream or something. But he turned back to see if we were following and motioned to make sure we were following him. I covered my mouth with the neck of my t-shirt, and Winnie grabbed my hand as we ran behind him, trying to keep our heads low.

In reaching the window, he gestured for Winnie and me to get out first. When I turned to grab Roo, my eyes locked with the soldier and confirmed what I knew deep down; it was Jesse. He didn't look ill anymore and appeared strong with no traces of his sickness. His dirty clothing and worn-out boots were now brand new.

In a split second, through the chaos surrounding us, his clear blue eyes contradicted the whole inky gray scene, bringing a feeling of peace and causing my rapid pulse to calm. The roaring of the fire, the blaring sirens, and the pounding in my head were all silenced, until I heard Winnie take a deep breath, and I knew she had felt it, too.

"My final mission," his mouth curved into a half-smile, but his eyes showed regret. I knew this was the last time I would see Jesse. "She's going to be okay," he said, and I believed him, even though Roo's limp body weighed heavy in our arms. "Believe," he nodded and let go, but leaned to my ear and whispered, "Betts, your grandmother said the ring is behind the radiator."

I wasn't sure what he was talking about, my mind was full of Roo, and I still believed I was in the middle of a dream.

Tears streamed down our sooty faces as we maneuvered Roo out of the window well. By that time, the fire department had come around to the back of the building and rushed over to attend to Roo.

Winnie and I were pulled away from the building and directed toward a waiting ambulance. "Is this your dog?" A fireman was holding a tired looking Skip in his arms.

"Yes, that's our dog," my chin quivered.

"We are going to check him out. Poor guy has been through a lot."

I bent down to take a deep breath of air and glanced beyond Skip to the window. There was smoke coming out of it, but that was all.

Winnie and I were taken to a second ambulance and immediately given oxygen, I strained my neck once more toward the window, but, by then, my parents and others had heard the sirens, and had come running. My mom stepped into the ambulance and wrapped her arms around Winnie and me.

"Roo, she's hurt! She's unconscious," I sobbed into my mom's shoulder, through the oxygen mask. She was too choked up to say anything, but gave me a tight squeeze, and let go, to rush over to Roo's ambulance, so she could hear what the medic was saying to my dad.

Winnie, Roo, and I were all taken to Shodair Children's Hospital. After a few hours of observation, Winnie and I were released. We sat in the waiting room with Karoline, Jack, and Duke for several agonizing hours into the night, waiting for news about Roo. When my parents finally emerged from her room, they reported good news, that Roo was going to be okay. She had a fractured ankle and a few mild bruises.

My dad chuckled, breaking the tension, "We knew she was going to be fine, when the first words she spoke were to ask if she was still going to be a flower girl in Karoline's wedding." We all laughed, and I may have laughed the hardest, because tears were spilling out of my eyes.

CHAPTER 23

When Roo was released from the hospital, she was told to lay on the couch for a few days and rest, mostly for my mom's own piece of mind that Roo would be safe and sound in our living room.

Roo's story revealed itself in the days that followed. She had chased Skip, who had chased the dog off the buffalo jump float. They ran all the way to the Seventh Avenue Gym, and on to the Central School playground. But, distracted by the swings, Roo forgot about the dogs and jumped on a swing, excited that she had the whole swing set to herself.

Upon seeing Roo flying out of her swing, Skip forgot all about his dog friend and turned his attention to Roo. Skip hated it when we were flying high on the swings. I think his dog brain believed his food source was in danger, and he would try to save us before we were fatally wounded and wouldn't be able to open his can of Alpo. He jumped and nipped at Roo, making it impossible for her to continue swinging, so she got off and started to head home.

As they walked by the old high school, Roo noticed the board was not covering the broken window and decided to peek inside the school. Skip was by her side and he immediately discovered the moldy peanut butter and jelly sandwich that Jesse hadn't eaten. In true Skip fashion, he bounded through the window in one jump and snarfed down the sandwich, baggie and all.

Roo yelled for Skip to come out, but we all know Skip's selective hearing issues, and she climbed in the window to retrieve him. After he finished the sandwich, he saw the soup cans, probably thinking it looked a lot like his Alpo dog food and clamped onto one with his teeth.

Roo said she got scared when Skip started growling and his hair stood up on his back. She tried to pull him back to the open window by his collar, but he was as solid as a statue, not budging an inch. And then, soup still in his mouth, he took off down the hallway, snarling like a rabid dog, nails scratching on the wood floor as he turned to run up the flight of stairs. Roo heard the can of soup fall down the stairs as Skip started barking furiously on the second floor.

Roo forgot her fears about ghosts, since her focus was to retrieve her dog, and she ran after him up the stairs.

Skip had cornered a cat that had jumped up on top of a bookcase, in one of the classrooms. The cat and Skip were at a stand-off, and Roo wasn't sure how she was going to get Skip out of the building.

Several minutes passed, and Skip started jumping against the old wooden bookcase, which made it begin to detach from the wall. The cat decided to make a break for it, but as it jumped, the ceiling high shelving unit completely detached from the wall and fell over onto Roo, pinning her to the floor.

She said she started crying because the shelf slammed down on her leg, which made Skip forget about the cat and he began licking her face. He seemed to sense she was in trouble and laid down next to her.

When the fire broke out in a classroom at the other end of the hall, Skip began whining, and wanted Roo to get up, but she couldn't. As the smoke grew thicker, she became disoriented and confused, and she remembers Skip's low growl as he laid his head protectively on her chest. The last thing she remembered before blacking out, was the glow of a bright light entering the room and kneeling beside her.

It was then her story took an intriguing turn. Roo was dead serious as she spoke, and we had no reason to believe she was lying. Everyone took it for granted that it was Winnie or me, who was kneeling beside Roo. But then she made a strange comment. "He was pretty," was how Roo described him.

"Do you mean handsome," since you think it was a man?" My mom asked, possibly alluding to him being a fire fighter.

"No, he was the prettiest thing I have ever, ever seen," Roo's arms were open wide to exaggerate the amount of prettiness. His eyes were bluer than the Specific and Atlantic Oceans. He had a pretty light around him, and his face was shimmering, like he washed in gold and pearls," Roo's eyes were big, and she was so certain about the experience that there was nothing we could do but believe her.

Winnie and I looked at each other. We had still not discussed the fact that Jesse had been inside the burning high school, not sure if we had been dreaming. Neither of us mentioned it to our parents or the police when they interviewed us, or anyone else, for that matter. Roo's description of his eyes matched my description of his eyes, but I didn't see any shimmering like she had described.

I don't know why, exactly, maybe we were still trying to protect him from getting in trouble, or maybe we were in denial because the experience seemed so unreal and out of this world, like a dream. People might not believe us. But, between Roo's account of the blue-eyed savior, and my emerging intuition that was trying to persuade me to believe the unbelievable, I was thinking maybe this was a case for Father Dolan, or a psychiatrist.

My parents, my mom especially, both knew something special had occurred in that building. They believed one hundred percent that some angelic being had blessed Roo and helped her survive the fire. They didn't care if anyone believed Roo, they believed her.

The following evening, after dinner, for once I didn't have to do the dishes. I think Duke and Jack had a weak moment and decided to give Winnie, Karoline, and me a break from dishes for one night. After all, we were being hailed as hometown heroes. We even received a call from the mayor and had an interview with the local newspaper. I was sure, the following night, things would be back to normal. We would probably have to save a whole school full of kids to get multiple nights off from dishes.

I went out on our front steps and had begun to

read my book, when a black shiny car pulled up in front of Mrs. Peters' house. Two army men, wearing their dress blues, got out of the car and headed to her front door.

My stomach was in my throat, thinking they had found Jesse. I swallowed a lump and wondered if he was sitting in the county jail but knew the answer to that. My eyes were glued to her front door, secretly hoping she wouldn't answer, to delay the news.

But she did open her door, and before they even spoke, her hand went up to her head and her knees gave out. They caught her as she was about to hit the ground and set her down on her porch swing. One of them took a knee by her side. As they spoke, I could see her shoulders trembling as she covered her face with her shaking hands.

I ran inside to get my parents. They hesitated at our front door when they saw the official military vehicle but proceeded to cross the street and join Mrs. Peters on her front porch. They all went inside and remerged about an hour later. My mom had her arm around Mrs. Peters' shoulders, while my dad talked to the men for a short time. Finally, they shook hands with my parents and Mrs. Peters, and left.

Mom stayed with Mrs. Peters' as Dad crossed the street back to our house, a solemn look on his face. "Did they find Jesse?" I asked, not sure I wanted to hear the answer.

He cleared his throat and said, "Yes. They did," he paused, and cleared his throat again, "they confirmed he was killed," he took out his hankie and wiped his nose.

"In the fire?" I choked, confused. He didn't appear to be affected by the smoke, in fact, he had looked

206

incredibly healthy.

"What do you mean, fire?" My dad gave me a confused look of his own. "He was killed in action. His squad was finally able to locate his remains in a dense forested area. He's coming home." My dad wiped his nose once more as I stared at him, my mouth was open wide enough to catch flies.

I was taken aback and sat down on the steps. Jesse was dead. In Vietnam. How could that be? Later, when my mom finally returned, she looked tired. She confirmed that Jesse's body was being loaded on to a plane in Vietnam, and he would be coming home.

I cried. We all cried.

That night, as Roo fell off to sleep, I turned to Winnie, "Winnie, that was Jesse that helped us in the fire, right? If that was Jesse, how did they just find Jesse's body an ocean away?"

"It was Jesse in the high school, I know it was him," she sounded confident.

"He told us to believe. Believe in what?" I asked.

"What do you believe? she asked.

"What do I believe?" I had an idea in my head about what I believed but forming the words to explain it, would make me sound looney. "What do you believe?" I asked her and rolled onto my back. My head swirled, and my eyes darted back and forth in the dark, looking for answers. This was one of those moments where words just couldn't explain the feeling. Something nagged at me, though. He said to believe, and even weirder he said...

I sprang to a sitting position. "Wait!" I suddenly remembered what Jesse had whispered in my ear. "Wait a minute," I jumped out of bed and ran and laid on my stomach, next to the radiator in our room.

"What are you doing?" Winnie whispered, looking at me and then to Roo's sleeping form to make sure she was still asleep.

I reached under the radiator and began to feel behind the leg. I didn't find anything and reached behind the other leg next to the corner of the wall. There was a slight indent where the carpet was cut around the leg of the radiator. I felt something round and had to keep poking at it with my finger because it was wedged in tight, but it finally popped out. I ran over to the closet and turned on the light, so I wouldn't wake Roo. Winnie got up and joined me.

I opened my hand to reveal a small gold band. "Grandma's ring," I whispered, wide-eyed. "This is Grandma's ring," I laughed, my eyes welling up. "I lost this ring when we were moving into the house, remember? I had almost forgotten…"

"Yes, I remember, you thought I had it," she smirked.

"Jesse," I started breathing hard and fanning my face in excitement, "Jesse said that Grandma told him the ring was behind the radiator. How would he know that? How could he talk to Gran…"?

Winnie closed the closet door and we slowly sat down on top of the shoes lining the floor, holding hands, cheek to cheek. My grandma had died when I was six, and my mom had given me Grandma's ring as a keepsake.

Grandma had been gone for four years now.

"If he talked to Grandma," Winnie whispered, "then... then..." she couldn't finish the sentence and put both hands on the sides of her head as though to keep it from exploding.

We sat back and stared at the ring, our minds racing. I put the ring on my finger and studied it, wanting it to tell me the story. Wanting it to be on Grandma's finger right then, her weathered hand enclosing mine.

We sat in the closet for several minutes wondering how something like this could be explained. We were in the middle of it, and still weren't sure what was reality. I took a deep breath and let it out. "Jesse spoke with Grandma," I whispered. There was something very comforting about that, like I had some kind of spiritual connection with Grandma, as though she had spoken to me from Heaven. Chills ran down my arm and I put a fist to my mouth not knowing if it was to contain my laughter or sobs.

We both crawled back into our twin beds and lay down facing each other. I touched the ring with my thumb, spinning it around my finger. "Winnie," I asked, "do you believe now?"

She let out a small laugh, "Yep," she answered, "do you?"

"Yep," I smiled. "Goodnight, Winnie."

"Night, Betts."

CHAPTER 24

When Jesse's body arrived in Helena, our family accompanied Mrs. Peters to the airport. We stood on the tarmac watching them unload his casket from the back of the airplane. Mrs. Peters stood small and fragile standing between my parents, and I was glad she had someone close by to hold her up in case she crumpled to the ground.

Jesse's casket was placed on the tarmac and two lines of men in their dress blues stood waiting for him, delivered a slow salute as the colors of the flag were unfolded to cover his casket. The call of orders broke the silence.

We turned around to follow the casket off the tarmac and I was taken aback to see hundreds of people from our town watching from afar. I heard Mrs. Peters gasp, as she placed her hand upon her chest, looking at the crowd of solemn faces of friends and strangers standing with their hands on their hearts, behind the chain link fence that separated the tarmac from the terminal.

They fell in behind us as Jesse's casket was loaded into the waiting hearse for the ride to the cemetery. A somber procession of headlights went on for a mile, winding its way through town to the Veteran's Cemetery at Fort Harrison, passing traffic cops who paused in their duties to salute. It was moving to find old men removing their hats, and ladies, girls, boys, all busy with their day, stopping to place their hands over their hearts when they noticed the winding river of cars.

Close to an hour had passed as we made the slow trek through the gates of the cemetery. Mourners circled Jesse's grave site as the military chaplain began the service. He spoke about Jesse's love of his country and especially the love and respect he had for his grandparents who had raised him since he was a child.

A veteran wearing an army jacket that had patches from WWII, came forward removing his VFW hat and shared a story about how Jesse would come by the local homeless shelter and help in the kitchen. "He never thought he was better than any of us." His voice revealed his age, reminding me of Walter Brennan from *The Real McCoys*. "Jesse made people feel important and that they mattered. If he noticed that someone needed shoes or a coat or something else, the next time he visited he would have a box full of clothing when he walked through the door. He was just a boy, then," he paused and pulled a white hankie out of his pocket to wipe his nose, "but that kid had the heart of a giant. Yes, he did," he nodded. He turned and toward the casket and proudly saluted.

One of Jesse's buddies told a funny story about Jesse during their time at basic training, and it felt good to laugh. He pulled off his baseball cap and nervously wrung it like a wash rag with both hands as he spoke, "Basic training turned our lives upside down, as you can imagine. Our drill instructors made sure of that," he smiled as he rubbed his chin and squinted to the sky. People in the crowd chuckled. "I think it was our third or fourth day at Fort Benning and we were in the chow line, given just minutes to get our food and eat, so of course we were hustling to finish before we had to fall in line. Well, after we snarfed down our food, we were cleaning up the area. For some reason, Jesse believed his cup of water was empty, and picked it up so fast, the water in the cup flew out over his shoulder into the face of the drill sergeant standing behind him. For a split-second, you could have heard a pin drop in that mess hall, and…" he paused and shook his head with a smile, "Jesse's eyes were bugging out of his head, praying he would live to see another day. He quickly grabbed some napkins and began dabbing the wet spots on the sergeant's unsmiling face and uniform…"

At that, the quiet chuckles in the crowd of mourners turned to full-fledged laughter. I'm not sure if he had more to the story, but his smile faded, and he walked over and laid his hand on Jesse's casket and straightened to salute, before he returned to his place in the crowd.

I needed that laughter to stop my kneecaps from shaking. I had asked Mrs. Peters if I could read a poem during the service, but didn't realize so many people would be attending, and it was my turn to speak.

I unfolded a piece of lined notebook paper that contained the poem and cleared my throat, "Jesse was my friend. He once rescued my dog and me during a huge snowstorm, and…" my voice cracked. I took a deep breath and wiped my nose with a tissue, blinking my eyes trying to stop the well of tears from filling. I smiled through the blur, "Jesse and I shared a love of poetry and I wrote this poem for him.

DAY IS DONE

Empty helmet stationed
on the barrel of his weapon,
inside a pair of war-torn boots
the laces pulled undone;
on sentry to his quiet frame
asleep in sweet repose,
the colors he had fought for
now protect and enclose
as a mother would a newborn child
a safe and warm embrace,
those colors would now shepherd him
to his final resting place.
Surrounded by the soil
that he fought fast to defend,
the rows of crosses
white on white
an army of guardians,
stand their ground on watch
o'er those who gave for others,
remaining at attention
for this newly fallen brother.
As rifles shatter the silence
their anger does resound
o'er the fallen comrades
who occupy this hallowed ground.
The bugle sounds its sorrow
to salute the fallen one,
day is done
my good friend,
day is done.
Day is done.

I gave my handwritten copy of the poem to Mrs. Peters. She squeezed my hand and whispered, "Thank you, Betts," her eyes glistened.

The chaplain concluded the service and the rifle volley sounded off, sending a flutter of birds skittering off into the horizon. I wasn't the only one to flinch as each shot rang across the field of fallen soldiers, and I imagined it a split-second snapshot of the deafening sounds of a battlefield. Afterward, it only took the bugler the first three notes of *Taps*, to cause the dams to burst. Sniffles radiated through the crowd, as the air filled with one of the few songs, guaranteed to make grown men cry.

My eyes wandered past the bugler, across the valley to the mountains beyond and rested upon the Sleeping Giant. It was a well-known mountain formation that formed just that, a sleeping giant. Now there would be another sleeping giant, I thought. Jesse had saved my sisters and I from that burning building. If he had not been there… shivers went down my spine.

Blinking my blurry eyes to focus, an osprey came into view. It began soaring in lazy circles high above all of us, just circling and circling, watching the service from above. I found Jilly in the crowd and motioned for her to look up. As she spotted it, a slow smile spread across her face. We both knew Jesse was free.

CHAPTER 25

After the service, our neighbors brought food and gathered at Mrs. Peters' house. Her living room was wall to wall with Jesse's high school friends who had dropped by and shared more stories about Jesse, that made us both laugh and cry. Former teachers and army buddies, and work friends of Mr. and Mrs. Peters, it was plain to see Jesse had touched many lives during his short stay here on Earth.

My dad and some of the other neighbors had noticed several repairs that were needed around Mrs. Peters' house, and planned to help spruce up the tired looking place. Mr. Gardner promised he would come over on Saturday to fix part of her fence that had fallen over during the last spring storm. My dad offered to look at her leaky faucet and change some of the burned-out bulbs that were too high for her to reach. By the end of the gathering, she had offers that ranged from helping in her garden to repairing the garage roof.

As everyone said their goodbyes, I knew Mrs. Peters was grieving for her grandson, but I sensed a hopeful feeling in the genuine smile that spread to her eyes as we said good night. Looking up at a black and white photo near the front door, of Jesse and Mr. Peters both grinning from ear to ear as they proudly held up a long string of trout, I nodded my head and smiled, knowing Mrs. Peters would be all right.

It had been a long and emotional day. When we got home, Winnie and I went out to the back yard, and laid on the cool grass under one of the apple trees. Skip had recovered from being in the smoky building and wandered over to plop his head on my stomach. His black wet nose nudged my hand for a pet, and I ran my fingers over the top of his head and down a silky ear, over and over until his brown eyes drooped closed.

Looking up at the night sky through the gentle flutter of leaves, my head was filled with the events of the past few days. I thought about Karoline, Jack, and Duke and their confrontations with the protesters, and the awful news about Oly Andersen. My mom having the courage to approach the station wagon full of kids and figuring out how to help them find their way home. They in return, giving me their cherished albums.

Losing Roo had been the scariest moment of my life, even scarier than going into the burning building. I didn't stop to think how dangerous it was to run upstairs into the smoke and fire, I just needed to get my sister out of there. Winnie staying with me, even though she knew the consequences, was the bravest thing she had ever done.

Jesse's death had shaken the town but also, had pulled people together to give hope to his lonely grandmother. I would always believe Jesse had returned to save Roo from the fire before his remains were found a continent away, but also, to make sure his grandmother would be okay.

Winnie, Jilly, and I, and hopefully Roo, would continue to keep Jesse's visit a secret until the time was right to share it. There was no doubt we would tell our parents and Mrs. Peters; they deserved the truth.

As if on cue, a shooting star flashed across the dark Montana sky, and Winnie and I followed its path until it disappeared into eternity. Usually I would make an instant wish for something like a new mitt or tennis shoes or shoot for the moon and say a million dollars, but for some reason, I couldn't think of a single thing I needed on this night.

As I lay there watching more stars emerge in the night sky, I could hear the familiar sounds of kids playing Kick the Can a street away, Mr. Magoo pounding out the dents in his garbage can, and a trio of dogs barking their annoyance in the distance. The chattering of sprinklers through the night air, still working to revive the brown grasses, the laughter of my brothers and their friends starting their cars to cruise the drag. *Get Together,* by the Youngbloods, was playing on Karoline's record player through her open window, mixed with the soft murmur of conversation and the clatter of plates and silverware as my parents cleaned the kitchen on the other side of the screen door.

Such a chorus of everyday sounds, most would not even notice their presence nor their significance. But these were the sounds of my town, the sounds of my neighborhood, like a warm quilt whose single stitched squares were as different in texture and color as can be, yet, sewn together as one, provided protection and comfort keeping me safe and warm.

Winnie sighed contentedly as she reached for my hand, intertwining her fingers with mine, squeezing ever so slightly. Skip's thumping heart, beat against my own as he burrowed his nose deeper into my neck, releasing his own long freeing sigh. Everything and everyone was in place. I squeezed my eyes shut letting a well of water escape, that left a trail of salt from my cheeks to the grass. So humble and content, so simple and sweet, these were the sounds of home.

The End

EPILOGUE

2017

"Time to go home," I reached for my grandson's hand, still holding the paper mosaic of the osprey in my other hand. I would frame that piece of art and hang it in a prevalent spot next to a Bob Morgan print of the Capitol building. Central School was no more, but I would always have my memories and this primitive artifact.

We headed down Warren Street past the Battlefield and the giant pine where my penny loafer had landed all those years ago. I was never able to retrieve the shoe and often wondered if it had become part of the tree after all this time. My grandson spied the grassy hill in front of the Cathedral and raced to the top, squealing and laughing as he rolled down the lawn. I stretched out in the cool grass halfway up the hill watching cotton candy clouds in the sapphire sky, memorizing my grandson's happy squeals to retrieve on a cloudy day.

Out of the blue, the piercing cry of an osprey drew my attention to one of the crosses at the top of the spires. Its shrill whistle repeatedly called out as it scanned the area below. My grandson paused to take notice and grabbed my wrist to look again at the artwork in my hand. "Nana, look, dat da birdie! He talkin' to us!"

I laughed and nodded, "Yes, he sure is talking to us." I squinted upward and whispered to the sky, "Welcome back, Jesse." Perched on the cross at the top of the spire, the regal bird was startled aloft when the bells began to toll the twelve o'clock hour. We watched him soar above Lawrence Street and make his way past Last Chance Gulch, over the mansion district, and toward the towering cliffs of Mount Helena.

"I'm hungry, Nana," my grandson broke my trance.

We continued the familiar tree lined walk toward my house, passing Jilly's white stucco house with the red trim, now occupied by a couple with three grown sons. It had been devastating news during our seventh-grade year, when her parents informed Jilly and her sisters that they would be leaving our neighborhood and moving across town. Our friendship dimmed for a while but never lost its fire and we continued to stay in touch throughout our lives. Duke and Jane ended up getting married a few years after Jane had graduated high school.

As for Mrs. Peters, we tried our best to help when she needed it, but as the years took their toll, she finally had to give up her little brick house.

I was a senior in high school the day a van from the local nursing home pulled up to her house. She was escorted out the door wearing her coveted fur coat and Mamie Eisenhower hat, even though it was early fall and the temperature hovered around seventy degrees. Mom,

Roo and I stood on our front porch, each of us swallowing the lumps in our throats, knowing it was probably the last time we would see Mrs. Peters. She glanced our way for one last look at the sitcom she had watched from her front window for well over a decade, and then raised her hand in a wave.

Mom and Roo went back into the house and I sat on the front step and watched the van's blinker signal a turn at the end of the street. I saw Mrs. Peters turn around for one last look so I raised my arm in a final gesture of friendship and called to her in a whisper, "Goodbye, Mrs. Peters, we hope you enjoyed our show."

ABOUT THE AUTHOR

Debbie Boyle is a poet, writer and artist living in Helena, Montana. Her hometown and the people in it, are the beloved backdrop for many of her poems and this first novel, *Sounds of Home*. Feeling like she hit the jackpot with her supportive family and a lifelong group of friends, Debbie's desire to intertwine and embellish bits and pieces of fond memories of her childhood, combined with imagination, compelled her to write this story about strength of family and the bonds of true friendship.

Made in the USA
Middletown, DE
06 November 2021